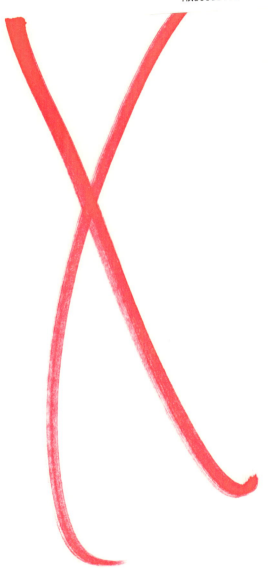

ZUBRICK'S ROCK

Zubrick's Rock

A Novel by
Robert Eringer

National Press
B O O K S

Washington, D.C.

Library of Congress Cataloging-in-Publication Data

Eringer, Robert,
    Zubrick's rock : a novel / by Robert Eringer.
       p.   cm.
    ISBN 1-882605-21-7 : ($19.95)
    I. Title.
PS3555.R48Z98 1995
813'.54—dc20   94-45325
                                            CIP

PRINTED IN THE UNITED STATES OF AMERICA

10 9 8 7 6 5 4 3 2 1

For Claire Elizabeth and Olivia Brooke

1

1297

François Grimaldi, known as Malizia to his friends, stood before the massive, solid oak gate and rapped three times with a heavy tree branch. He took a deep breath and looked down to the bay, now in darkness.

"Who calls?" cried a voice beyond the gate. "Identify thyself!"

"Please, I am hungry," answered Malizia. "I have traveled many miles. I need food and rest."

"And who be you?" boomed a voice from the other side.

"François Crovetto. I am a monk. Please, sir, I beg you."

The gate creaked open a few inches. One guard raised a lantern; two others squinted for a look at the bearded François, dressed in a brown hooded monk's smock. They did not notice he wore boots instead of humble sandals.

"I am hungry and thirsty," pleaded Malizia. "Please find it in thy heart to feed me this night."

The gate opened wider. The guards gestured him in. A shrill animal voice distracted the three guards momentarily. With well-rehearsed grace, Malizia drew a long sword from inside his cloak and in one swing decapitated the gateman, then turned and punctured the chest of the second guard in one powerful thrust. A third guard, holding the lantern, froze momentarily in shock, then turned and ran. Malizia quickly caught up, hacking at the man's right side until he collapsed, breathing hard, face up, begging for his life. Malizia stood over him, whispered a prayer, then plunged his sword into the man's heart.

Malizia raced back to the partially open gate. He whistled softly and pushed his weight against the gate to open it wider.

From behind bushes and trees, Malizia's small army advanced, rushing through the gate and into the fortress that was Monaco. Their strike was well-planned; they knew their way around. First they attacked the guardhouse, only two men on duty during the dinner hour. Both were slain.

Malizia led his men into the palace, skewering guards who dared stand in his way; others threw down their swords and ran. He strode directly to the dining room, where Adolpho Spinola was enjoying a Provençal feast of lamb, roasted on the spit, and goat cheese.

"You!" yelled Spinola. "What are you doing in my home? Explain thyself instantly!" Malizia was Spinola's arch rival on the Ligurian coast.

"Ah," said François, his men taking position at points around the room. "This is *my* home."

"You cannot do this!" yelled Spinola. "They will come from Genoa to put you out."

"It is done," said François. "*You* are going to Genoa. I will permit you safe passage if you leave within the hour."

About 700 Years Later

Barry Zubrick looked at the letter before him on his desk. He had just collected his mail, as was his custom at 2 p.m., from the Poste Restante box only 500 yards from his home. The letter was in French, typed on official stationery and decorated with the red and gold crest of Monaco. Despite having lived in the tiny principality for six years, Barry could not speak nor read French. On the rare occasions he ventured out to restaurants, he dined only at touristy dives whose menu was bilingual.

Barry half expected the letter, intuitively understood its meaning: Barry's presence was no longer desired in the principality. He expected it, yes, but it did not lessen the blow.

Barry put down his bifocals, leaned back in his cushioned desk chair—more of a sag than a lean—and swiveled around for his floor-to-ceiling picture window view of the Place du Casino and the Belle Époque Hotel de Paris, the epicenter of Monte Carlo—and the tranquil Mediterranean Sea beyond.

Why was it the more money he mustered, the less freedom he had? Barry wouldn't return to the United States for fear of being plunked in jail for ignoring certain demands from the IRS. He couldn't return to England for similar reasons. And when he recently applied to Ireland for part-time residency, they turned him down flat. The world was growing smaller and Barry, though growing richer each day—$26,753 just from money market interest—was growing weaker. Years of hypochondria had finally evolved into a variety of genuine illnesses, from chronic dyspepsia to vertigo, giving him the opportunity to tell his doctors, "See, I was right."

Barry lived in constant dread that the U.S. Marshals Service would find out where he lived, kidnap him and swish him to a maximum security prison, probably in Marion, Illinois, of all places.

It was Barry's radical views that got him into trouble, rather, his implementation of those views. Barry was morally opposed to taxation and he objected to subsidizing "corrupt" governments. And in Barry's world view, *every* government was corrupt. Barry reserved his greatest contempt for the United States, of which he was a citizen, though he held six passports from different countries and considered himself no one's citizen, a native of the world, answerable to no one. Certainly not the American government which, he felt, depending on his mood, was composed of thieves, bureaucratic bunglers or conspirators.

Barry had a knack for hooking himself to bad people. Or the other way around. They would come to him— if they could get past his Poste Restante accommodation address—and try to hook him; dip into his fortune to finance their idealistic projects, nicely tailored to suit Barry's own ideologies. Hustlers on the make. Yet if they got past his mail drops and fax machine, Barry was a light touch. He could be extremely hard-crusted when writing a fax, but in person he was mister milquetoast, and he knew it, and that is why he hid behind his fax machine for 98 percent of his dealings with the world beyond his Monte Carlo sanctuary.

Barry Zubrick should have been hiding the day he met Gary Lincoln.

It had taken Lincoln almost 18 months and scores of letters to wangle a meeting. But his persistence paid off. The pay-off, following Lincoln's slick pitch, began with Barry's 20-grand donation to Lincoln's *Patriot Report* newsletter; it evolved into a full blown organization they formed in partnership called "Liberty is Us." Barry put up a hundred grand to wage war against the Big Brother conspiracy. And Lincoln quickly used the dough to fly first class to London, Washington, Paris, Johannesburg, Bonn, Houston, Milan, Nice... staying at Claridges in London; the Ritz in Paris... all, he told Barry, to present the "right image" as he tried to cajole additional funds from wealthy conservatives. After the grand tour, it was time to milk his subscribers, to whom Lincoln served up Barry's name as an appetizer, and from whom thousands of dollars more poured in.

The problem was this: "Liberty is Us" didn't *do* anything. When the charge card bills arrived—at least two Concorde flights; hand-made custom shoes from John Lobb, three Savile Row suits—the "Liberty is Us" account was drained, overdrawn, and Lincoln faxed Barry, pleading for more cash.

Barry faxed back in Barry-speak, a phonetically-inspired style he liked to use, especially when annoyed:

U R asking 2 much. Plez send full accounting immed.

Lincoln tried to call, but Barry had changed his telephone number again, a ritual he practiced every three months.

Meanwhile, a reporter from the *Miami Herald* had been telephoning Lincoln's office in Melbourne, up the Florida coast. Bill Blade, of the *Herald*'s investigative unit, had been monitoring Lincoln's newsletter for months, letting it simmer on a back burner, and now he was poised to nail down his story. It came from a *Patriot Report* copy editor, a badly-paid Lincoln staffer who held an ambition to become a big city reporter and was delighted, when Blade called him at home a month earlier, to get his foot in the door at the *Herald*. And take a whack at his autocratic boss at the same time!

Gary Lincoln took Blade's third call, and was staggered by Blade's depth of knowledge about him. Blade knew Lincoln had gone bankrupt twice, had been married three times, had beat his wives, and even that he played German march music on Sundays. Word was, Lincoln was a closet Nazi, disguising his beliefs with a veil of populism. And now, Blade asked, was it true that Lincoln had wheedled subscribers—plain ordinary folk—of their hard earned pay under the "Liberty is Us" banner and simply spent the money on himself?

"Well, that's not true," said Lincoln, breaking his own first rule of dealing with reporters. You *never* answer them on the spot. You listen to their questions, say you're in a meeting and promise to call them back, thus giving you time to ponder the questions and come up with a reasoned, properly elusive response. "I have been active around the world on 'Liberty is Us' business."

"Yes, let me see here," said Blade. "Shoes from John Lobb, thirteen hundred and fifty dollars plus 75 dollars' shipping. Panther watch from Cartier in Paris, twelve thousand dollars... Lunch at Le Gavroche, four hundred and seventy-eight dollars... Would you like me to go on, Mister Lincoln?"

"Mister Blade, I don't know where you get your information, but I can assure you..."

"Mister Lincoln, I'm reading from your American Express statements."

Lincoln went silent. He wasn't sure whether to blow

his stack for this invasion of his privacy or hang up. Instead, looking at Barry's fax—it annoyed the hell out of him—he said: "Look, it wasn't my idea. `Liberty is Us' was created by Barry Zubrick, the millionaire investment guru in Monte Carlo..."

Lincoln made a strong case, painting Zubrick as the villain, and Blade wrote it all down in shorthand on a yellow legal pad, smiling with self-satisfaction: his story was no longer simmering; it would be tomorrow's main dish.

Blade clacked a few keys to access the computerized clipping file, then punched in the letters B-A-R-R-Y Z-U-B-R-I-C-K. A selection appeared for Barry D. Zubrick; Blade hit the enter key.

A 12 year-old article from the *New York Times* appeared. It described Barry as a 52 year-old multimillionaire investment consultant, an American who lived in Switzerland and sometimes associated himself with libertarian causes. The gist of the piece was that Barry had attempted to start his own country on an island near Australia. He raised thousands from private clients and supporters, and the scheme went bust. There was no picture of Barry; he had refused to be interviewed for the article, which noted that he was "reclusive." It went on to say that Barry had something of a cult following among fringe right- and left-wingers who, some said, were so far around the bend that their beliefs were compatible. He was, said the piece, a whiz on metals, and he charged two thousand dollars an hour for his financial advice.

That was all.

Blade read over his notes a third time, then touch-keyed the phone number Lincoln had given him for Zubrick. The dull European tone rang twice, followed by the whistling twang of a fax signal.

Blade put the phone down, made a copy of the New York Times article, punched himself a clean screen and composed a fax to Barry Zubrick:

Dear Mr. Zubrick:

I am a reporter for the Miami Herald and I am writing a story on "Liberty is Us." I interviewed Gary Lincoln this morning and he gave me your number. I would like to ask you a few questions for the sake of accuracy. Please fax me your telephone number so that I may phone you. (315) 555-6382.

Blade transmitted the fax and waited. An hour later a copy boy walked over to Blade's desk with a fax for him. Blade read it:

Dear BB:

LiU is a private matter, has nuthing to do with U.

If U write about it or me, I will Su.—BZ

Blade shook his head and laughed. This Barry Zubrick was quite a character.

It took Blade the best part of the afternoon to knock out his piece. It made page three in next morning's paper, under the heading BARRY ZUBRICK NAMED IN FRAUD SCAM, linking the "reclusive mega-bucks Barry Zubrick of Monte Carlo" to Florida con-man Gary Lincoln.

Burrells' Clipping Company of New Jersey picked up the *Miami Herald* piece as part of the regular service they performed for the Monaco Information Office in

New York City. The office mostly promoted tourism for the principality. It also operated as Monaco's eyes and ears in the United States, an unofficial embassy.

The *Miami Herald* article on Barry Zubrick turned up in an envelope with assorted gossipy tidbits about Monaco's royal family, the Grimaldis, from *People* magazine and a slew of tabloids. Blade's piece was immediately deemed the most interesting item in the weekly batch by Frank Salvatore, a former New York City cop who had been a bodyguard to Monaco's royal family when they visited the United States, and now coordinated Monaco's security matters in North America.

Salvatore faxed the article to police headquarters in La Condamine, the port district of Monaco, where it was logged and channeled to the Bureau d'Etranger, the authority that administrates Monaco's foreign residents, who outnumber native Monegasques five to one.

The article was marked for the personal attention of Pierre Chantelot, the bureau director, whose very name made most foreign residents look over their shoulder. It was Chantelot who personally conducted interviews with would-be residents, and it was Chantelot who would re-interview residents each year for three years to determine if their presence was beneficial to the principality. And it was Chantelot who personally decided if an applicant for residency should be turned down or if a renewal be refused. Rarely did Chantelot terminate a residency midstream, but it did happen from time to time if a resident was thought to be giving Monaco a bad name.

Chantelot read the article and asked his secretary to pull their file on Barry Zubrick, which he perused over expresso and a croissant at the Café Dauphin Verte, a short block and a half from headquarters.

Barry Zubrick was already borderline, at best, in Chantelot's mind. He had survived the scrutiny of three renewals only because of the millions, 90-plus, he had on deposit at three Monaco banks, and because he actually *lived* in Monaco, a lifestyle many residents tried to avoid. Most of them used Monaco for its income tax-free address; lived in fear Chantelot would catch on and revoke their papers. There were other small, quasi-independent countries where tax exiles could claim residency and stash their cash, but all were less desirable than Monaco, a jewel on the French Riviera. It was an iron-clad rule with Chantelot that residents should live at least six months of the year in the principality to be eligible for renewal. He asked residents to bring their telephone and electricity bills to the interviews for an assessment. Many residents had caught on, and they hired maids to visit their apartments once a week to turn lights on and off and to run up the telephone bill. But almost every apartment building in the principality had a concierge and it was the concierge's job to sort mail, hold keys for emergencies— and to secretly cooperate with enquiries from Chantelot's bureau.

In some ways, thought Chantelot, Barry was a model resident. Kept to himself, never had disputes with Monegasque plumbers or electricians, paid all his bills promptly. But Monaco could not tolerate having its good name soiled by an alleged con-man. Monaco was vigilant about keeping Monaco free of sleaze. And if they let Barry Zubrick stay, what kind of example would it set? If he made an exception in Barry's case, someone worse might follow.

Monaco was sensitive of its image as a gambling paradise. It relished the paradise part, but it loathed to be compared to Las Vegas or Atlantic City. Its network of worldwide information offices were urged to de-emphasize casino gambling, to point out that less than five percent of Monaco's income was derived from the casinos.

Chantelot took a last sip from his cup, wiped his bushy mustache and left 11 francs on the table. He looked up Rue Princesse Caroline to the Tete de Chien, part of the French Alps that surround the principality, and marveled at the pink reflection bestowed upon it by the sun. Another beautiful day in Monaco. He walked to his office and instructed his secretary to draft a letter to Barry Zubrick.

2

arry Zubrick looked again at the letter signed by
Pierre Chantelot from the Bureau d'Etranger, then
around his cluttered office: investment newsletters
and financial magazines were piled high; a whole library
of books, mostly economics, with a strong dose of conspiracy theory; trophies and award certificates from
strangely-named fringe groups. What a pain in the dokus
it would be to move everything—and to where? Northern
Europe was out of the question; frail Barry caught a cold
just *thinking* about Switzerland and Germany and Bel-
gium. The choices in southern Europe had pitfalls. Barry
demanded total efficiency in the amenities around him—
telephone, fax, mail, computer services—so he had long
ago ruled out Portugal, Spain and Italy. No, it looked to
him like he would have to leave Europe altogether. The
upside was it would then be even harder for his enemies
to find him—and Barry liked to imagine he had very
many more enemies than he actually had. South Africa
was a possibility; Uruguay, another option. He looked out
his window again. The azure Mediterranean was so peaceful—an idyllic setting for himself. Damn Gary Lincoln!

Barry picked up the phone and called his lawyer,
Alan Bennett, an Englishman who practiced in Monaco.

There were a handful of English lawyers and insurance brokers in the principality, and all were either incompetent or corrupt. Bennett agreed to meet Barry at 4:30 in the lobby of the Metropole Hotel, a 90-second sprint from Barry's apartment. Barry never met people at their office. He assumed they would bug his conversation, or maybe set a trap of some kind. Blackmail weighed heavily on Barry's mind. And no one, but no one, was allowed to visit Barry's apartment—he never gave out his address. Not to his lawyer, his stockbroker—no one. Barry conducted his business with others only in hotel lobbies, and he rotated between four such lobbies within five minutes' walking distance of his apartment building. Ah, Monaco, so easy.

The Metropole Hotel's lobby was spacious with marble pillars and ornate painted ceilings and sparkling crystal chandeliers, newly built to blend with Monte Carlo's Belle Époque style. And, most important to Barry, the lobby was always empty, like a mausoleum most of the time.

Barry arrived first, sharp at 4:30, and he was briefly annoyed with Bennett when the lawyer turned up seven minutes late, which Barry visibly noted on his wristwatch, lest Bennett think of starting his meter earlier.

Barry was never one for small talk; socializing bored him, a complete waste of time. He thrust the letter from the Bureau d'Etranger at Bennett.

Bennett pulled a pair of reading glasses from his coat pocket and adjusted them on his bulbous, veiny nose. He read slowly and deliberately, in no hurry to hasten the meeting. Like most lawyers, Bennett charged by the minute, and his firm charged Barry twice the normal rate.

Bennett whistled softly.

"What does it say?" Barry demanded.

"I'm awfully sorry, but you've just been declared persona non grata, old chap."

"I know, I know. Does it say *why*?"

"I'm afraid it doesn't. The letter says you have 45 days to put your affairs in order and that you must return your carte de séjour and your Monegasque car plates before your departure." Barry almost never drove, but he kept a Range Rover greased up in the basement car park of his apartment building for an escape over rugged terrain come the apocalypse. Barry believed a worldwide financial collapse was always around the corner, followed by a social collapse and rampant civil disobedience.

A waiter appeared from out of the frescoes to take an order. Barry glanced up at him suspiciously; a spy, no doubt.

"Bonjour," said the waiter, and waited.

"I'd like a cup of tea," said Bennett, "thé au lait, si vous plait."

"Just water," said Barry.

"Evian, Badoit?" asked the waiter.

"I don't care. Evian, I suppose." Barry rolled his eyes in annoyance. He liked the Metropole because it was impossible for a waiter to hover at another table, listen in to his conversation. This obvious spy was making a nuisance of himself.

The waiter jotted onto his pad and left.

"What can we do about this?" Barry asked Bennett.

"I don't think we can do anything," said Bennett, shrugging. "There is no appeal system for revocation of residency."

"Can't you *talk* to them, find out if there's been a mistake?"

"I suppose it wouldn't hurt to call and inquire," said Bennett, realizing he had only 44 days more to milk this valued client.

"Maybe they'd like me to make a donation," suggested Barry, "to one of their foundations or charities?"

This intrigued Bennett; his firm could slice 15 percent off the top.

"Let me take this letter back to my office. I'll make a copy and return the original, and I'll call the Bureau d'Etranger first thing in the morning."

Barry opened a file in front of him. "I've already made you a copy." He handed it to Bennett.

"Where will you go?" asked Bennett. "To live, I mean."

Barry rubbed his eyes with an open palm. "I don't know. It's darn difficult to find a place with good communications and a climate like this. And Nice airport only 20 minutes away..."

The waiter returned with a tray. Barry drank his water in two gulps and got up to leave before Alan had taken his first sip of tea. Business was over. And Barry wasn't about to pay for Alan Bennett's tea break. Damn Englishmen—all they ever do is drink tea on someone else's nickel.

Barry walked the long way back to his apartment, through the park and around the corner onto Boulevard des Moulins, just in case Bennett's curiosity got the better of him.

The New York stock exchange, six hours behind, was still open. Barry tried to distract himself by focusing on the day's buying and selling. His heart was not in it.

Barry's Filipino maid fixed him a Nicoise salad and

he went to bed by nine, lulled to sleep by CNN business news.

Barry rose early the next morning. Among the faxes that had accumulated during the night was one from Gary Lincoln, asking, again, for more money to clean up the overdraft left by "Liberty is Us."

"The alternative," wrote Lincoln, "is that I declare bankruptcy—and this might mean further media coverage."

Blackmail, again, thought Barry. The price one paid for great wealth.

Barry could not contain himself past ten. He called Bennett's office. Bennett had not yet arrived, said a secretary. Barry hung up and cursed. Nobody ever worked anymore, not even on weekdays. Barry fired off a missile to Bennett—"Call me immed—BZ"—and pushed it through his fax machine.

Just before eleven, a fax from Bennett hummed through Barry's machine:

Dear Ted: Have spoken with the bureau. Please call me.

Even Bennett did not have Barry's phone number. And he had learned to be discreet in his faxes to Barry, using the code-name Ted. Barry assumed that his fax machine was bugged by at least three intelligence services.

Barry telephoned Bennett, said, "Let's meet where we met yesterday, in 15 minutes."

Barry wasn't sitting when Bennett arrived, but hovering just inside the revolving door. "C'mon," whispered Barry. "We'll talk some place safer."

Bennett looked around the Metropole lobby—there wasn't a soul in the place, for God's sake!

Barry led the way down to Loews and they took a table at the far end of the expansive piano bar, an extension of the modern lobby.

"So?" whispered Barry.

Bennett shook his head. "They had nothing to add to their letter. They said it was no mistake."

"Can't we appeal it?" asked Barry

"They said there is no appeal process."

"Can't we go see them?"

"They said it would mean nothing. The decision has been made and will not be reversed. You know what the French are like. The Monegasques are worse."

"They can't do that!" yelled Barry. "I've been here six years. They can't just throw me out at a month's notice without an explanation!"

"I'm sorry," said Bennett. "But they can. Years ago they threw out Lady Docker the same way. No explanation. But it was rumored that she tore up a little Monegasque flag and threw it on the floor in front of diners at the Hotel de Paris. If I may ask, have you done anything like that lately?"

"No. It's an abomination. What will happen if I refuse to leave?"

Bennett did not pry further, though his curiosity was piqued. "I expect they would arrest you and confiscate your apartment. I would not recommend that course of action."

"Well, what *do* you recommend?"

"Sell your apartment. If you like it here so much, buy a place in Beausoleil." Bennett chuckled to himself. Beausoleil, a French town bordering Monaco, was literally across the street, and most of the time the mayor was communist.

Barry puzzled this for a moment. "Any tax implications?"

"Of course," Bennett counseled. "You would become subject to French income tax—about 30 percent these days."

Barry did some quick mental calculations; his brain was the only agile muscle in his body. It would cost him three million dollars each year to live in Beausoleil. Eight thousand, nine hundred and eighteen dollars a day!

Barry didn't see money in relative terms—a buck was a buck, pure and simple. And he wasn't about to pay France 17,500,000 francs for merely sleeping on their soil, breathing the leaded fumes of Peugeots and Citroens. Governments could be so demanding of him. He was a citizen of the world. What right did governments have to tax him, to regulate him, to police him? Governments were self-possessed with preserving their own power, increasing their power, not serving the people. Governments were as artificial as borders—regions carved up at whim by empirists without regard to natives. Empire-building had no place in Barry's ideal world. Small was not only beautiful, but the only efficient way for people to govern themselves. That's why he liked Monaco, a sovereign, self-governing state only one square mile with a population of 30,000. That's why he liked the idea of starting his own country. It had almost worked 12 years before—an unpopulated island with no resources. Australia had almost accepted his ten million dollar bid. Barry's island would no longer be subject to Australian law. Barry would be its ruler; maybe build a casino for income; issue collectors' postage stamps and currency—graced with his

own face! It all looked so rosy. Two days before settle-
ment, a reporter found out about the deal, raised a ruckus
and prompted an investigation. It had cost Barry a million dollars in expenses, plus a few strategically placed
bribes to politicians. Elected folk didn't like to go up
against the media. Conviction has its limits.

"No," said Barry, returning from his thoughts. "Beausoleil is no good. Any other ideas?"

Bennett shrugged. "I wish there was a silver lining to
this cloud, but I've yet to find one. I am dreadfully sorry.
Let me know if we can be of any assistance in closing
your affairs here. Would you like me to retain the services
of a real estate agent?"

Barry flashed Bennett a look of disgust; already trying to make money out of his misery. "I think I'll be able
to handle that myself," sniffed Barry.

"I'm just trying to help," said Bennett, holding up
his hands in mock defense. "You don't have much time."

It was true. Forty-four days to sell his apartment,
pack and transport his furnishings, do something about
his Range Rover.

"I need some air, I'll call you if I need you." Barry
didn't say thanks. Thanks for what?

Bennett sat impassively. He'd miss Zubrick's money,
but he sure wouldn't miss *him*.

Barry rose and said goodbye. Bennett did not extend
his hand, knowing Barry did not approve of shaking
hands—"spreads cold germs more efficiently than screw-
ing," he'd say.

Barry took the elevator up to the Loews roof-top
exit and walked into the brilliant sunshine, about 62
degrees on this March day.

He turned, poised to walk through a tunnel toward

Place du Casino, the general direction of home, but paused, looked up at the sky, and continued across the Loews roof terrace, towards the port. For the first time in months, Barry was going to take a walk. Doctors had been advising him for years to walk every day, if only for 20 minutes. Barry viewed that advice contemptuously; walking with no destination was a complete waste of time. Period.

But on this day, Barry was in no rush to return to his home office and face the unpleasant task of packing or dealing with Gary Lincoln's blackmail. He needed to think—think up a new home, somewhere.

Barry walked down Avenue Ostende to the port, where two dozen large yachts were berthed, and along the promenade adjacent to Boulevard Albert 1st in La Condamine, which had more a feel of a French town than the glitz of Monte Carlo. Most tourists who visited the principality believed Monte Carlo was all there was to Monaco, and Barry, even after six years of living in the principality, thought the same.

Barry walked around the port, down the Quai Antoine, past the Monaco Yacht Club, to which he had never been—Barry didn't give sports a moment's notice— and up some steps to the jetty. He had a mind to walk out to the lighthouse at the far end of the jetty, but Barry impulsively followed a path that curved the other way, disappeared around the back of the Rock. He followed the path around, had it to himself, enjoyed the solitude. Monaco was always buzzing with activity—tourists, new construction—but behind the Rock there was quiet; a sheer drop to the sea below. It wound through two tunnels, and then a lobby-like terrace built into the Rock with cafes and souvenir stands, and an auditorium which, every hour, played *The Monte Carlo Story*, a slide-show, for tourists.

Barry took an escalator up. It deposited him on the Rock, Monaco Ville, outside the Jacques Cousteau Ocean-ographic Museum. Barry had never set foot on the Rock. It was so different from the rest of Monaco. Peaceful. Good air. Cooler. He cut into one of the tiny streets and was amazed to find a medieval village, narrow, winding streets, no cars. He walked until he reached the Princes' Palace, a faded-pink structure at the far end of the Rock. The Monegasque flag was flying above the palace, which meant the prince was in residence. Barry was in time to witness the Changing of the Guard, a ceremony that unfolded every morning at 11:55 to entertain the hordes of tourists, who stood in the expansive, cobblestoned square in front of the palace and then bought postcards and plastic souvenirs at a row of small shops that conve-niently lined the courtyard. It was amusing to Barry that the palace guard consisted of but eight white-uniformed, helmeted carabiniers. That was Monaco. Small. Small minded. Barry's chuckle turned into a growl.

Barry turned around and walked down Rue Basse. He was getting tired, unaccustomed as he was to such demanding exercise, and he paused to rest outside The Historical Wax Museum. He was hot and he assumed it would be cooler inside, maybe air-conditioned, so he paid 20 francs and entered the museum.

The exhibition of 24 wax figures of Grimaldis through seven centuries began with the story of Malizia's ouster of the Spinolas in 1297.

Barry studied and re-studied the simple French text. His heart began to beat faster, adrenalin pumping. Barry Zubrick's agile brain was storming.

3

Alec Perry answered the door at his modest three-bedroom house in Bethesda, Maryland and signed for an overnight business letter from DHL.

Though unexpected, he had an inkling who it was from. DHL was France's answer to Federal Express. And one glance at the return address—"Ted, Poste Restante, Monaco"—confirmed it was Barry Zubrick.

Alec was a former CIA operative whose 21-year career in the clandestine service had come to an abrupt halt after he killed a terrorist—one of those suspected of torturing William Buckley, the Beirut station chief who was kidnapped in the early '80s and who died at the hands of Hezbollah.

Alec hadn't meant to kill the man, not initially, anyway; just knock him around. But the Arab taunted him, practically admitted his role in the Buckley murder. Alec couldn't help himself. He had served with Buckley, learned everything he knew about tradecraft from Buckley—he had spent Christmas, celebrated anniversaries with the Buckley family. And then watching the awful video—a despicable video of the actual torture... the Arabs believed in an eye for an eye, and Alec was willing to oblige.

When he came face to face with Abdul Hafez, something inside Alec snapped. It took but one swift rabbit punch in between Abdul's eyes to dispatch a tiny bone deep into the Arab's brain, killing him instantly. More merciful, thought Alec, than how Buckley had met his end. Every time he thought about it, lamenting his estrangement from the agency, Alec came to the same conclusion: if he had it to do over, he'd do the same again.

The agency booted Alec out after a fast, secret investigation; the Senate Intelligence Committee wanted the Justice Department to prosecute him, but finally conceded to agency pleas to keep the matter hushed up and classified.

What irritated his superiors was that Alec showed no remorse. No, he hadn't meant to kill the Arab. But, no, he wasn't sorry it happened. Alec was lucky to walk away with his 20-year pension. He had long ago used up whatever goodwill the agency may have had toward him. He wasn't a team player. A maverick who wasn't happy in an embassy among bureaucrats, Alec preferred deep-cover assignments, working on his own.

Alec had served in a variety of foreign posts. When President Reagan secretly concluded that the success of Solidarity in Poland was crucial to the overthrow of communism in Eastern Europe, Alec was dispatched to Warsaw, ostensibly to research and write a book. His undercover work assisting the Solidarity underground earned him a Distinguished Intelligence Medal.

But after the Hafez "incident," the brass at Langley quickly forgot Alec's successes and remembered him only as a troublemaker—and the staff psychologists were instructed to tighten their entrance exams to more efficiently weed out "non-conformists."

Alec went through a long period of decompression—
outright depression at times. Secret work was what he
knew, what he was good at—and there didn't seem a role
in the world for an ex-spook. He talked to a few executive head-hunters who sought him out and wanted to sell
him to Kroll or Hill and Knowlton, the likeliest homes
for ex-CIA, FBI and Secret Service types. It seemed old
spooks didn't fade away, they set up shop on K street,
consulting for Third World countries on how best to take
advantage of the U.S. government. Or how to circumvent
red tape and buy arms for people *trying* to be Third
World countries.

A handful of literary agents and publishers called
Alec periodically in search of "memoirs," but he didn't
have a book to write. Nothing he could say would get
through the CIA's review board anyway.

Alec did what Alec did best: kept a low profile,
waiting for the funk to lift. But Alec's son and daughter
were in college, and he was having a rough time trying to
support the extremely high cost of a four-year liberal arts
education. He had some cash saved, about 20 grand, and
the mortgage on the house in Bethesda was nearly paid
off. His wife had died two years earlier—lost to ovarian
cancer—and the house felt lonely. Once he got his footing
straight, Alec planned to dump the house and all its
memories, maybe rent a condo in Georgetown.

Alec had signed up for an investment seminar in
Aruba, a way to combine an educational experience with
a dose of winter sunshine. Maybe he would learn a little
something about money; like how to make it grow faster
than the cost of living.

And that's where Alec Perry had met Barry Zubrick.
Through John J. Stemmer, the controversial, recently-re-

tired four-star army general who had liaised with Alec in two hemispheres and had, as a kid, attended high school with Barry Zubrick. The mutuality led to dinner for three, during which Barry offered Alec some pointers: get your savings out of U.S. dollars; get them into ECUs, a theoretical currency devised of a smattering of European currencies. Not only was the dollar expected to weaken severely, but ECUs paid more than twice as much interest as dollars. You couldn't lose.

Currency trading was Barry Zubrick's forte, to which he had graduated from precious metals. Barry had amassed his initial fortune in the early '70s. It was illegal, for many years, for American citizens to own gold, but Barry had discovered Switzerland, and he was impressed by Swiss ways. The Swiss, always serious about money, were perennial believers in making gold a large slice of their portfolio. Barry desired to be rich, so he studied the habits of those who took money seriously.

He bought gold when it was still $35 an ounce, and he borrowed heavily to buy more. When President Nixon took the U.S. dollar off the gold standard, the yellow metal spiralled upward, first to over 150 bucks an ounce, and then, a few years later, to over 600 dollars an ounce. That's when Barry got out of gold, at its peak, and moved into currencies. It amused him that most Americans could not see beyond the U.S. dollar, yet there were a dozen other currencies worth possessing, speculating upon, especially when the dollar was strong and other currencies could be bought cheap. Then back into dollars when the dollar went bearish. And Barry discovered that though the currency market was influenced by political events and bank policy, it was *driven* by currency traders, who made sure, for their own survival, that currencies went up and down, in cycles that Barry found challenging to predict. And that's what he did 14 hours a day—trends and theories, charts and patterns. Barry liked to socialize with numbers, not people. He played with numbers, danced with them, and finally created ways to turn small numbers into large numbers. Numbers, numbers and more numbers. The method to Barry's madness was focus in its purest form.

The two men—Alec and Barry—got on well. Barry was impressed by Alec's CIA background. He gleaned from General Stemmer, in confidence, the scoop on Perry's fall from grace, his maverick tendencies. Barry liked what he heard. He needed a man in the United States, preferably Washington, who could do things on his behalf, since Barry never set foot on U.S. soil. Things as trivial as buying and forwarding newly published financial books. Or handling quasi-legal problems that seemed to find Barry, however much he tried to hide himself.

Assured by General Stemmer of Alec's total discretion, Barry met with Alec when the three-day seminar ended and made his pitch: go on retainer for me—$500 a week—and handle small assignments from time to time. Expenses paid. Extra money for larger assignments. No contract necessary. Just a verbal understanding. Alec liked the casualness of Barry's offer, and could sure use five hundred bucks a week. He agreed.

A month later, Barry paid for Alec to fly to Monaco for a visit, and Alec utilized the occasion to open an account at Barclay's Bank in Monaco and exchange his dollars into ECUs. The two men met in the lobby of the Hotel Metropole to discuss Alec's first big assignment.

"They're planning to kidnap me," Barry whispered.

"Who?" asked Alec.

"The U.S. government—they want to kidnap me and take me back to the United States, confiscate my money, throw me in jail."

"Why?"

"Why? Because they don't tolerate independent thinkers like me, that's why! Because they think I owe them money—the buggers!"

"Do you?"

"Do I what?"

"Do you owe the government money?"

"They *think* I do."

Alec began to understand he was dealing with an eccentric. In Aruba, surrounded by other investment gurus, Barry Zubrick came off as fairly conventional. But on his own turf, Barry allowed his peculiarities to run rampant. Alec looked at him, amazed, wondering if this was why Barry had flown him 4,000 miles, to tell him the U.S. government wanted to steal his money and kidnap him.

"I have an important assignment for you," Barry whispered. "I want you to find out what their intentions are toward me and what they're planning."

"Who?" asked Perry.

"The U.S. government. What their plan is. What they know about me. Where they feel they can most easily grab me."

"Um-hum." Perry nodded, doing his best to disguise a grin, suddenly realizing that Barry was probably half-cracked.

"And in addition to the five hundred I pay you each week," added Barry, "I'll pay you five thousand dollars for your report."

Alec gulped. Half-cracked—but *rich*.

Barry reached into his inside jacket pocket and pulled

out a checkbook. "Would you like the whole amount up front?"

"Ummm, let me go back to Washington," said Perry. "Ask a few questions—make sure I can find out what you want to know."

They agreed that Barry could simply wire the funds to Alec's new ECU account at Barclay's bank, and Alec gave Barry the account number and wiring instructions.

"Is that all?" Alec asked. He had been in the principality all of four hours. "How about dinner?"

"Dinners are a complete waste of time," sniffed Barry. "The New York markets are still open. But I have tickets for the circus tomorrow. Let's meet right here, the Metropole, at 7:30 sharp, evening, of course."

Each year in February, Monaco played host for one week to an international circus festival. The finest acts from around the world gathered to compete for prizes.

So Alec had hung around overnight and through the next day. He poked his head into the casino, watched the action for a half-hour, but didn't indulge; he wasn't a gambler. Alec walked and walked, as he always did in a new place. Not only was walking his favorite form of exercise, but this was how he learned about a new place, exploring side streets and taking note of shops and services.

Next evening, Alec was at the Metropole at 7:15. It was ingrained in Alec to be 15 minutes early for a rendezvous. Alec always had a plan, a contingency—an exit, if necessary—and you couldn't have a plan unless you were familiar with your immediate surroundings.

Alec and Barry went to the circus. Barry marveled at the lion tamer and acrobats and applauded wildly.

During intermission, Barry took Alec outside the tent to one of the many refreshment vendors and bought two hot dogs. Barry smothered his dog with sweet relish and mustard and made a complete mess of his hands as he munched the snack. Gooey condiments ran down his wrists. To Alec's utter astonishment, Barry pulled his shirt from his trousers and wiped his hands on his own shirt-tails, then tucked them back into his pants.

When he looked up and saw Alec staring at him, Barry raised a finger and said, "That's what shirttails are for." And he was as serious as colon cancer.

Alec had returned to Washington and called Ron Moloney, a long-time friend and former chief of the U.S. Marshals Service. It was the Marshals Service that was charged with hunting down American fugitives outside the United States.

"Ever heard of Barry Zubrick?" asked Alec. "He lives in Monte Carlo. Do you know if he's a wanted man?"

"I'll check it out for you. Do you have a few days?"

Moloney telephoned Alec the following day. "The Marshals Service has never heard of Barry Zubrick. Who is he?"

"Oh, just someone I met. No big deal. Thanks, Ron.

It was just as Alec had thought. Nobody was after Barry Zubrick; nobody in the Marshals Service, anyway.

Alec faxed Barry that a report was forthcoming, and Barry wired five thousand dollars to Alec's account.

Alec knew that Barry would never believe that the U.S. Marshals Service had never heard of him; he'd probably be downright offended. And then he'd start to think that Alec was part of the plot, recruited by the Marshals Service to entrap him. So Alec wrote a report that said the U.S. government had no immediate plans to kidnap Barry, but merely monitored his residency status from time to time to update their file on him. That, Alec reasoned, would put Barry's mind at ease without deflating his ego or suspecting a double-cross.

Barry accepted Alec's report without a word.

In the months that followed, Barry frequently faxed Alec for minor matters—to send sea-sickness pills by courier, mail an occasional magazine, order up a company search from Dunn & Bradstreet—and Alec was content to earn 26-grand a year for what probably averaged out to one hour's work a week.

And suddenly, thirteen months since their meeting in Monaco, here was a DHL overnight business letter from "Ted." And it probably meant a second big assignment.

Alec took the large stiff envelope to his desk and opened it. Inside was a single page, typed. It said:

> URGENT—Find out hu R the living descendants of the Spinola Family that was ousted from Monaco 700 yrs ago by the Grimaldis. Do not fax info—courier only.

Alec puzzled over the assignment. Barry sure was kookie. But hey, you never had to send him a reminder about payment. His weekly transfers were timed to a Swiss clock.

Alec would need a genealogist, but that was no problem; Barry never objected to expenses or sub-contracting. Barry was content for Alec to be a middleman, a coordinator, so that he did not have to deal with others personally, get his hands dirty. Barry liked to deal with as few people as possible. And if Alec handled things, it meant Barry's name wouldn't be bandied around either.

Alec knew of a reliable firm of genealogists—Pitkin and Miggles, Ltd.—in Henley-on-Thames near London.

The agency had once contracted with them to plot the family tree of a Southeast Asian ruler, though this had been brokered for them by MI5, the British Security Service, which had in turn used its own cover.

It was only 11 a.m., still time enough to telephone London, five hours ahead. Alec called a long-distance information operator and netted the number of Pitkin and Miggles. He touch-keyed the number direct and set a fresh legal pad on his desk in front of him to record expenses.

"Hello?" A clipped English accent answered the phone. "Pitkin and Miggles."

"Yes, I'd like to speak with either Mister Pitkin or Mister Miggles," said Alec.

"I'm afraid Mister Pitkin is deceased. But I will see if Mister Miggles is available."

"Thank you," said Alec. "Please say it's long-distance from the United States."

"Right-e-ho."

There was a pause of about 30 seconds.

"Hello, Miggles here. How can I help you?"

"Ah, Mister Miggles. My name is Alec Perry. I'm a writer and I'm researching a historical novel. How difficult would it be to trace a family from the thirteenth century to the present?"

Miggles blew heavily into the phone to preface his response. "Extremely difficult. But we've done worse. I must tell you, though, it is an awfully expensive proposition. Are you looking for advice on how to do this yourself, or do you wish to commission our firm with the task?"

"I hadn't thought about doing it myself. What are the pros and cons?"

"We find that many amateur genealogists enjoy this as a hobby. But it can take many, many months for a novice to find and study the records one must consult to put a family tree in order. We, on the other hand, have over 75 years' experience at this craft, and we possess a library full of the appropriate reference books and family crests. However, it is not an inexpensive undertaking, and as a writer the cost is quite probably a concern to you."

Pitkin and Miggles were accustomed to offering a personalized service to aristocrats and the moneyed-class. Not would-be novelists.

"What kind of cost is involved?" asked Alec.

"We have an hourly rate of 50 pounds plus expenses, which can be substantial. The project you have in mind could cost upwards of five thousand pounds, depending on expenses. Where does this family originate?"

"Monaco."

"Ah, that could be problematic. Through the centuries, Monaco has fallen under French, Italian and even Sardinian protectorship. And the name, if I may ask?"

"Spinola."

"I'll say this—it's Mister Perry, is it?"

"Yes."

"I will consult several standard reference works, Mister Perry. And if you would be kind enough to telephone me this same time tomorrow, I will provide you with a more detailed proposition. Is that all right?"

"Splendid," said Alec. The English art of articulation was catchy.

Then Alec composed a fax to Barry Zubrick:

Dear Ted:

Courier pack received. Assignment may take

some time—maybe a month or more. Will be expensive—outside consultants needed— between 10 and 20 thousand dollars. Please advise.

Barry's response was immediate:

TILT: Month no good. Must have info in 10 days, earlier if pos. No later. Expense ok.

Alec shook his head. Barry, Barry: impatient as always—expense a minor detail.

Alec telephoned Mr. Miggles the next morning at 11 a.m.

"Yes, good afternoon Mister Perry—or is it morning?" said Mr. Miggles, not bothering to wait for an answer. "Your family, the Spinolas. They were a Genovese family, an important family, merchants, and they ruled Monaco up until the 1290s. This is good news. It is easier to trace a well-known family than an obscure one, obviously. But it will entail a trip to Genoa, I'm afraid. Air and hotel accommodations for the best part of a week. If that is satisfactory, along with the hourly rate I mentioned yesterday, we could begin next week and deliver a report to you within four to six weeks."

"I can't wait that long," Alec blurted. "I mean, my deadline is near. Couldn't you do it any faster?"

"The time frame I have given you *is* fast," said Mr. Miggles.

"But couldn't you put additional people on it, start sooner, today?"

Mr. Miggles laughed a good hearty laugh. "It's already tea-time today, I'm afraid. And we're rather booked up."

"What if I pay extra," said Alec. "Could you do a 'rush job'?"

"Yes, I've heard that colonial colloquialism—you chaps over there are always in a hurry. But we don't rush anything around here. It is a painstaking business, Mister Perry. We don't just consult telephone directories."

"Is there *any way*," said Alec, "we can speed up the process without interfering with your quality service?" A little flattery couldn't hurt.

"How soon do you require our report?" asked Mr. Miggles.

"Ten days."

"The best I can do is this: I will put one man on it tomorrow, Wednesday, and put a second man on it beginning next week, dispatch him to Genoa. We'll do as much as we can in ten days. It may not be conclusive, but you never know what may turn up."

"Thank you, Mister Miggles. We have a deal."

"Let me pass you to my secretary, Mister Perry, to take your details. As you are calling from overseas, we will require a deposit."

"Of course, Mister Miggles. No problem."

******

A Fed Ex parcel arrived at Alec Perry's door from London exactly two weeks later. And not a moment too soon. Barry Zubrick had sent three faxes venting extreme impatience the previous three days, and when Barry wanted to be cranky, he was king.

Alec opened the envelope with a pair of desk scissors and pulled from it a neatly typed report from Pitkin and Miggles, Ltd.

The report began with the Spinola family crest, then
detailed the family's proliferation through five centuries.
It stopped in the 1780s. The conclusion read:

> The direct line of Adolpho Spinola, who once
> ruled Monaco in the late thirteenth century, ends
> in 1783. However, if one were to count first, sec-
> ond and third cousins, male and female, there are
> literally hundreds of Spinola descendants in the
> world today, many of whom possess different sur-
> names through marriage. Our past research into
> families of Genovese origin shows that the most
> likely concentrations of Spinola descendants are
> to be found in northern Italy—it was not a custom
> to move south—and the USA, more specifically,
> the northeast coast.

It made sense to Alec, and he hoped this was what
Barry Zubrick wanted to hear. Alec wrote a short fax to
Barry—"Material in hand—will courier today"—and he
telephoned Federal Express for a pick-up. Fed Ex guaranteed a two-day delivery.

*****

Barry Zubrick picked up the Fed Ex parcel from his
Poste Restante address at the main post office in Palais de
la Scala. Excited, he rushed back to his apartment, cutting
through the back entrance of the Hermitage Hotel, out
the front, and through Le Sporting d'Hiver, pausing by
the cinema, ostensibly to read which movies were playing,
trying to detect any hint of surveillance. Satisfied he was
not being trailed, Barry whizzed into his apartment building, into the elevator, and up to his sixth floor apartment.

Barry tore open the envelope, glanced at the heading, then turned straight to the conclusion. He read Pitkin and Miggles's round-up.

"Holy Malola!" yelled Barry. "I waited two and a half weeks for this?"

The Filipino maid scurried out. In a *good* mood, Barry was difficult.

When he calmed down, Barry leaned back in his desk chair and read the 15-page report from beginning to end. A solution began to germinate in his mind. And Barry typed out new instructions for Alec Perry.

*****

Two days later, another DHL van appeared in front of Alec Perry's house. Alec signed the delivery man's clipboard, opened the stiff envelope and read Barry Zubrick's short letter:

> Plez place classified ad in Wall St. Journal, under "announcements." I want it to say: "SPINOLA—Genovese origin—Family reunion planned. Write..." Get PO box to use as accomo address. Urgent. Plez do immed. Today.

Alec shook his head in amusement. Why was Barry so interested in Spinolas. An investment scam? Obviously, Alec didn't have a need to know, and Barry was more vigilant with that rule than most of Alec's former colleagues at the agency.

Alec drained a cup of freshly-brewed black coffee and drove to Glen Echo post office, a small, country-style post office only ten-minutes' drive from his house. He filled out a form, paid 15 dollars in cash and was given

a key to Box 684. On his way home, Alec stopped at a
7-11 on River Road and picked up a copy of the *Wall
Street Journal*. He studied the classified ad section, noted
the telephone number on his legal pad and touch-keyed.

A telephonist transcribed the ad's wording from Alec
and took his American Express details for payment. The
ad would run once only, in both the national and international editions.

Alec faxed Barry to say the deed was done; that the
ad would appear in two days.

Alec checked Box 684 two days after the ad appeared. It was empty. And nothing the following day. But
the day after, a single envelope appeared in the box, hand-
addressed, sporting a printed sticker in the top left-hand
corner announcing that the letter was from:

> Dr. Gerard Spinola, D.D.S.
> 2155 Washington Street
> Hoboken, NJ 07030

Alec didn't open the letter. He sealed it in a Fed Ex
business envelope and arranged for it to be collected that
afternoon for express delivery to Monte Carlo.

Barry Zubrick could not contain his enthusiasm upon
receiving the Spinola letter. He picked up the telephone
and dialed Alec's number. Alec was stunned to hear Barry's
voice, a most uncommon occurrence.

"Uh, hi Ted," said Alec. "Did you receive my package?"

"Yes, yes," said Barry. "That's why I'm calling. I want
you to call that dentist in New Jersey—you know who I
mean?"

"Yes. Spi . . ."

"Shhhh!" Barry admonished. "Look him up in the

phone book, call him, invite him to visit me, all expenses paid."

"But Ted," said Alec. "What if he wants to know *why?*"

"Make something up, anything, I don't care. There's no time for couriers and I can't explain over the phone. Find him and bring him with you to see me."

"When?"

"As soon as possible. Tomorrow, the next day, no later."

* * * * *

Alec Perry would have liked more time to plan; re-search Gerard Spinola, D.D.S. and his habits; come up with a plausible story custom-made for the dentist. Instead he'd have to wing it. But Alec prided himself on winging it through tense, complicated situations. And so, assuming a reasonable-sounding plan would hit him somewhere between Washington and Hoboken, Alec packed a garment bag for a four or five night trip—one business suit, one navy blazer—and caught the Delta Shuttle from National Airport to LaGuardia.

Alec didn't dwell on a plan—he simply let his mind wander, let his imaginative sub-conscious take over and, at 22,000 feet, an idea struck: Alec would tell Dr. Spinola that he had a client in Monaco who desperately needed Spinola's dentistry skills. He would say it was an emergency, and coax the dentist to join him on that evening's Delta flight from JFK to the French Riviera.

Alec grabbed a cab at LaGuardia, by-passed Manhattan, around to Hoboken. The cabby let him off on Washington Street, a block from Spinola's office. It was already close to three o'clock; Delta's flight departed at 7:50.

Alec walked into the shabby, run-down office building and consulted the directory. Dr. Spinola was on the third floor. It was a walk-up; no elevator. On the third floor Alec found an old wood and glass door, on which was etched the words "Gerard Spinola, D.D.S." He knocked and entered the small waiting room. It didn't look like much; was as drab as the lobby downstairs. A few vinyl covered chairs, ragged copies of *Sports Illustrated* and *Highlights*.

A homely, bespectacled receptionist in a nurse's smock sat behind a small counter, talking loudly on the phone with a thick Jersey accent, admiring her long polished red nails.

Alec waited till she finished her call, approached the counter and asked, "Is Doctor Spinola available?"

"Do you have an appointment?" The receptionist studied Alec's bland looks.

"No. I must see him about an important matter."

The receptionist let her thick glasses droop down her narrow nose and, looking over them, eyed Alec suspiciously.

"Are you a debt collector?" she asked.

"Nope."

"His wife's new lawyer?"

"No." Alec laughed. "Nothing like that. I need Doctor Spinola's assistance for a patient overseas."

The receptionist's jaw dropped. "Are you sure you have the *right* Doctor Spinola?"

"Yes, quite sure. Is he here?"

"Are you for real?" asked the receptionist.

"Yes, it's true," said Alec, feeling less sure about his cover legend.

"Hold on a minute." The receptionist rounded a corner out of sight.

After a couple of minutes, Alec saw a little head pop out from around the corner and pop back when Alec returned the gaze. Then an entire body appeared. A short, wiry frame, hair slicked back, thin beard, goatee at the chin with a pencil thin moustache. He must have been 45 or 46, and was trembling. The figure gestured Alec with an arm wave to follow him out the door, into the hall.

"Are you Doctor Spinola?" Alec was puzzled.

"C'mere, c'mere," said the figure, whispering. They were both standing in the seedy hall. "Tell Joey I'll have the ten grand on Friday. I promise, I promise. Friday."

"Are you Doctor Spinola?" asked Alec.

"Yeah, yeah. Who the hell you think I am? Just tell Joey I'll have his ten grand. I don't want no trouble."

"Doctor Spinola, I don't know what you're talking about and I don't know who Joey is. I need to talk to you. Can we go back inside?"

"Yeah? Joey didn't send you?" Spinola heaved a sigh of relief. "Yeah, yeah, let's go back inside." Spinola had a nervous twitch on one side of his face, and it was twitching up a storm. He looked both ways quickly and gestured for Alec to re-enter the office.

"Whattaya want?" asked Spinola, wiping his sweaty forehead with a handkerchief.

"I have a client in need of emergency dental treatment. You were recommended to him."

"Me?" said Spinola. "Fine, where is he, send him in."

"Doctor, he is in Monte Carlo in the south of France. He wants you to come see him."

"What?"

"My client wants me to escort you to Monte Carlo to give him emergency treatment. He'll pay your expenses plus a good fee."

"Why me? Are you sure Joey didn't send you? Is this some kind of joke?" Spinola's face was twitching again.

"Please, Doctor Spinola. I'm serious. You were recommended to my client for your skillfulness at dealing with abscesses." This was getting difficult. "He doesn't trust French doctors."

"What you say your name was?"

"Alec. Alec Perry."

"Alex, I treat mostly welfare patients, fillings, pulling rotten teeth. Are you sure you've got the right dentist?"

"Doctor Spinola, it might sound strange, but I'm telling you the truth. You have been recommended to my client and he is willing to fly you to Monte Carlo for a few days, business class, and pay all your bills, plus a healthy fee for your trouble. My client is a very wealthy man."

Spinola thought for a moment. "Will he pay me ten grand?"

"Hmmm, he didn't tell me the amount," said Alec.

"Well, I've got a whole appointments book full of patients I'd have to cancel."

Alec wondered where they were.

"But for ten grand I'll do it," Spinola added.

"I can't guarantee that high a fee on my own."

"Then forget it," snapped Spinola. "This sounds fishy anyway. I've got work to do." Spinola turned to leave.

"Wait a minute," said Alec. "Let me call my client, see if I can establish a fee."

"As long as you use a credit card," said Spinola. "My long-distance service was cut off."

"Actually," said Alex. "I need to send a fax. Do you have a fax machine?"

"Are you nuts?" said Spinola. "There's a photocopy shop down the street that has a fax, if it's working."

Alec took a piece of typing paper and scribbled a message for Barry:

Am with your pen pal—he will only come if you pay him $10,000.

"What's the 'phone number here?" asked Alec.
"201-555-6905," said Spinola.
Alec wrote down the number, and added:

Please call me in 10 minutes to confirm the arrangement.

Back at Spinola's office, Alec waited near the phone. It rang, the receptionist answered and handed the phone to Alec.

"What the hell does that dentist want ten thousand dollars for?" barked Barry Zubrick.

"I think he needs to pay off a debt," whispered Alec. "He won't come unless he's promised that amount."

"All right, all right. Just get him here, fast."

"We're already booked on tonight's flight—we should be there by eleven tomorrow morning. You want us to stay anywhere special?"

"I'll make the booking at Loews. It'll be under your name only. I'll call you at 11:30."

"Got it," said Alec.

Dr. Spinola peeked out his surgery; Alec replaced the receiver to its cradle.

"Okay," said Alec. "You're on. Ten grand."

"You mean it?" said Spinola. "Half now."

"What?"

"Half up front—then I'll know you're serious."

Alec shrugged, pulled a checkbook from his jacket pocket and began writing.

"Whattaya call that?" said Spinola.

"Call what?"

"That." Spinola pointed to the checkbook.

"I call this a checkbook," said Alec.

"I gotta have cash," said Spinola.

"I don't have five thousand in cash!" Alec protested.

"Okay, gimme part cash."

Alec always carried five one hundred dollar bills tucked away in his wallet, a holdover habit from his agency days when he traveled a lot, never knowing where he might find himself; a cash contingency, bribe money. He pulled his wallet from a back pocket, rummaged around and found the neatly-folded bills.

"I can give you five hundred now, the rest by check or when we arrive in Monaco."

"Done," said Spinola, reaching for the bills.

"Just a second," said Alec. "You got a passport?"

"Yeah, yeah, sure," said Spinola.

"Where is it?"

"Upstairs," said Spinola. "I got an apartment upstairs."

"Well go up and pack a bag, for three or four nights, and don't forget your passport. I'll give you the cash when you get back."

Spinola faced his receptionist. "Miss Petronelli, duty calls." He turned to Alec. "Do I need any instruments?"

"Nah," said Alec. "You'll be able to use a dental office in Monte Carlo."

"Okay." He turned back to Miss Petronelli. "Cancel everything the rest of the week and watch the fort— we're outta here."

4

Dr. Spinola returned to the office from his upstairs apartment dressed in colorful plaid slacks, an open-neck silk shirt, a cream-colored sport coat and white loafers.

Alec grimaced. "I hope you have a suit in there." He pointed to Spinola's scuffed garment bag, of no identifiable origin.

"Yeah, yeah, don't worry," Spinola grabbed five bills from Alec's grasp. "Are we goin' or what?"

Alec checked his watch. It was close to 5 p.m. "Let's move. Can we call a cab?"

"Nah, there's always one at a rank downstairs."

Down on Washington Street there wasn't a cab in sight; Spinola hadn't counted on rush hour. It was almost dark out. And sleeting.

They returned to the office, telephoned three cab companies, who promised nothing.

"I'll call my cousin Vinnie," said Spinola. "He'll drive us to Kennedy."

Vinnie pulled up in a beat up, 15 year-old Buick; Alec and Spinola were waiting in the lobby.

"That's Vinnie, let's go!" Spinola jumped into the front seat; Alec climbed in back.

"Hey Jer, where youz guys going?" shouted Vinnie, big, unshaven, smelling of garlic. He looked at Alec suspiciously. "Vinnie Esposito, nice to meet ya."

"A pleasure," said Alec.

"So where youz goin'?" asked Vinnie. He didn't wait for an answer. "Ya know, Joey's been lookin' for you."

"Yeah, yeah. If Joey calls, tell him I'll be back in a few days—with his money."

Vinnie scratched his head, cursed the traffic. "I've got a tip at the Meadowlands tonight. Johnny-come-Lately in the third. Whatta name for a horse, huh?"

Spinola dug into his pocket, pulled two bills and held them up for Vinnie. "Do it."

"Where youz guys goin'?" Vinnie asked for the third time, pocketing the cash.

"Monte Carlo," said Spinola.

"Well, *excuse me*. What the hell you gonna do in Monte?"

"Duty calls. I'm needed for emergency treatment."

"*You?* Someone needs *you?* Gimme a break!"

"Shaddap-a-ya-face!" yelled Spinola. "Who the hell asked you anyway?"

Vinnie hit the brakes; they squealed as the car skidded, and the driver in the car behind hit his horn.

"Show a little respect, huh? You're lucky ya gotta cousin like me who'll haul your ass on a night like this!"

"Yeah, yeah," said Spinola.

Traffic was atrocious, but Vinnie made it to the Delta Terminal at JFK just after 7 p.m. Alec rushed to the ticket desk, picked up two business-class tickets, and the two men ran to the gate where passengers were already boarding the aircraft.

"Damn, can't we stop at a bar?" asked Spinola.

"Don't worry, they give you a drink in business class as soon as you're on board."

They took their seats on the Airbus 310. A flight attendant immediately offered champagne or orange juice. Spinola downed three tall glasses of champagne before the aircraft had taxied to a queue of planes waiting for take-off; Alec drank one mimosa.

Spinola sat back in his roomy seat, relaxed. "What's this guy's name?"

"Who?" Alec was absorbed with his thoughts.

"The patient. What's his name? What's wrong with him?"

"Barry Zubrick. I told you, he's got an abscess."

"Why come to me?"

"If I knew, I'd tell you." Alec was wondering the same thing himself. Why bring this fool to Monaco? And since he didn't have any answers, he really didn't want to talk about it. The trip, with Spinola's fee, was going to cost Barry over 20 thousand dollars. That would cover a year of college for one of Alec's kids. Alec wished he had money to burn like that. He wished he had money just to cover his *bills*.

Once airborne, Spinola threw back three large scotch and Coca-Colas, and drank another half-bottle of champagne with dinner, which he hardly touched. And then he was out, snoring like a horse, as if each breath he expelled was his last. He was still out when, 45 minutes before landing, Alec stirred him awake.

"Ohhhh, man," said Spinola. "I think I'm gonna heave. Where the hell am I?"

"We're almost in Nice," said Alec. "You'd better throw some water on your face. You look terrible."

Spinola pulled himself from his seat, reached for his

hold-all and pulled from it two tablets of codeine. Ah, sometimes it made all the sense in the world to be a dentist, even if he was sick of looking into people's mouths, blood everywhere. And the American Dental Association putting out a new guideline every week for AIDS prevention. Now they were recommending autoclaves, an oven for baking dental instruments. Another five grand out the window. Who was going to pay for *that*? Not his welfare patients, that's for sure. There's no question, Spinola thought as he locked himself in the toilet, if he had it to do over again, he'd have been a broker, trading stocks. Or worked at the track. He still cursed the day his Uncle Angelo put him into practice after first buying his passing grades.

Spinola looked into the mirror and saw a gray-green complexion and bloodshot eyes. He massaged his cheekbones and used the toiletry kit, complimentary of business class, to brush his teeth and carefully shave around his thin beard and moustache. "Oh fuck," he muttered, "they don't even give you Visine."

Spinola grabbed a glass of water from the galley, threw back the codeine and staggered back to his seat. Alec looked at him, shook his head. "Are you all right?"

Spinola burped. "What time is it?"

"Just past nine a.m.," said Alec. "Better sit down and fasten your seat belt—we're almost there."

Spinola went quiet, eyes closed, holding his head, waiting for the codeine to take hold. Lately, it seemed, his head was always aching. Alec looked out the window at the Riviera; the jet made its final approach into Nice-Côte d'Azur Airport.

The pair glided through Immigration, passports stamped, and out the terminal to the a taxi stand. A cabby in a Mercedes beckoned them.

"Bonjour, monsieur," said Alec. "Monaco, si vous plait. Hotel Loews."

"Oui, Monsieur," grunted the driver, and they were off.

Of four routes to Monaco from Nice, a 12-mile drive, the cabby chose the Moyen Corniche, a fast, mountainous route that curved around the French Alps, through tunnels, affording a spectacular view of the coastline below.

Before long, the cabby was zipping at 90 kilometers an hour, overtaking slower drivers and handling curves as expertly as a Grand Prix race-driver.

Spinola was green again, tugging at Alec's arm. "Tell him to slow down—I feel sick."

Alec smiled, "Don't worry, he's a good driver, probably does this ten times a day. We'll be there soon."

Spinola started to roll down the window, but didn't make it. He upchucked against the glass, and it splattered back at him and dribbled down the door.

"Jesus Christ!" yelled Alec.

"I told you I was going to heave!" Spinola wiped his mouth with his sleeve.

"Sacré Bleu!" hollered the cab driver, watching the commotion in his rear view mirror, and he cursed in French the rest of the way to Monaco, then caused a scene on the forecourt at Loews Hotel, prompting two valets to jump in, siding with their newly-arrived guests. Alec was quite prepared to pay extra to clean the Mercedes, but the driver wanted to vent his rage anyway, complaining that it would take an hour to clean his car— lost time.

All eyes were upon Alec and Spinola as they walked through the lobby to the check-in desk.

"You really know how to arrive in style," said Alec.

Spinola belched loudly and held his forehead with an open palm.

"I told you I was going to be sick," said Spinola.

"So it's my fault. If you hadn't drunk so damn much on the plane you wouldn't be sick."

"I gotta sleep," said Spinola.

The pair registered under Alec's name and surrendered their passports, a Monaco law, to be logged into a hotel computer that linked to a central system at police headquarters. An envelope awaited Alec, and the receptionist handed it to him. Alec turned aside, tore open the envelope and found ten five-hundred dollar travellers checks. The dentist saw them, too.

"Is that my dough?" Spinola peered over Alec's shoulder.

Alec peeled one traveller's check from the pack, folded it and put it inside his jacket. He handed the rest to Spinola. "Now you happy?" Over Spinola's shoulder he thought he saw General J. J. Stemmer standing outside the tabac fifty yards away. No, couldn't be.

Alec and Spinola were given two rooms, side by side, on the fourth floor, each with a private terrace overlooking the sea.

"Sleep it off," said Alec, as they exited the elevator. "I'll call my client, tell him we're here, and we'll meet him later today."

Spinola mumbled in agreement and disappeared into his room.

Alec liked Loews. The room was cheerful and spacious, the bathroom functioned efficiently and the TV had CNN. It was a particular delight of his to lounge on the terrace. He neatly unpacked his garment bag, took a shower, shaved, and waited for Barry Zubrick to call.

The phone rang at 11:30. Alec picked it up.

"Ah," said Barry. "You made it. Is the dentist with you?"

"Of course."

"Can we meet at twelve, usual place?"

"I can, the dentist can't. He's hung-over and gone to bed."

"Doesn't he realize I'm calling the shots? Doesn't he have any personal sense of responsibility?"

"No, on both counts. He knows less about why he's here than me, and I know zilch. He thinks he's here to fix your mouth."

"What?"

"I'll meet you at twelve," said Alec. "We need to talk without him anyway. Then we can re-group later in the afternoon."

Alec quickly jumped out of his bathrobe into a blazer and khaki trousers. He wandered out the hotel, up Avenue Speluges and through the Galerie Metropole, a three-tier shopping center with marble staircases and crystal chandeliers out of *Gone with the Wind*.

Alec took the final escalator up and stood in front of the Hotel Metropole. He walked through its revolving door at precisely noon, and Barry appeared simultaneously, having entered though the rear exit that faced his apartment building.

They sat down in the frescoed mausoleum, beneath seven glittery chandeliers, as they had one year before, enjoying, again, the whole ornate lobby to themselves.

"He's safe, isn't he?" asked Barry, by way of a greeting.

"Who, Spinola?"

"Shhhh!" Barry held a finger to his lips. "Don't say

his name. Let's just call him 'The Dentist'—that's the code. Got it?"

"Got it." Alec wondered who could possibly overhear them in the huge, empty lobby.

"When can I meet The Dentist?"

"I'd guess he's going to sleep most of the afternoon," said Alec. "He was in pretty bad shape—puked all over the taxi coming in."

"Is he sick?"

"He's worse than sick," said Alec. "But, in particular, he had too much to drink on the plane. Somehow, I get the impression it wasn't unusual for him."

"He's here," snapped Barry. "That's what's important. And what was that you said about fixing my mouth?"

"He's a dentist. The only plausible story I could come up with to get him over here was telling him you have an abscess, that you need emergency treatment, that you don't trust French dentists and that he was recommended to you."

"Why did you tell him that?"

"What was I *supposed* to tell him? That you're trying to organize a reunion for the Spinola family?"

"I'm surprised he believed you."

"I don't think he did. He's a nickel and dime dentist in a run-down practice. Nobody in their right mind would recommend him for *anything*—and he knows it. He just needs ten grand—he owes a gambling debt. Now, are you going to tell me what's going on? Why, for instance, you wanted me to bring that horse's ass to Monaco?"

"The man you call a horse's ass," said Barry Zubrick, "is going to be the next Prince of Monaco."

5

"Wait a minute, let me get this straight," Alec laughed. "You are going to take over the Principality of Monaco and install that, that *dentist* as its ruler?"

"Exactly," whispered Barry. "Return Monaco to the Spinola family, its rightful owner."

"You're not serious, are you?"

"Of course I am. Look at how the Grimaldis stole Monaco from the Spinolas 700 years ago. They just marched right in and took it by force. Well, now the Spinolas are gonna march back in the same way and take it back—by force."

"But those kinds of things just aren't done anymore," said Alec. "You didn't have international law back then, a UN..."

"And we shouldn't have them now," barked Barry. "They're part of the conspiracy."

"What conspiracy?"

"The One-World-Government conspiracy that's trying to first unify Europe and then unify the world and turn us all into numbers processed by a computer and monitored by Big Brother. The Trilateral Commission, the

Council of Foreign Relations, the Club of Rome— those scoundrels are all in it together!"

"And just supposing you march in, kick out the Grimaldis and call Spinola the new prince. What do you suppose France will say about that? Monaco exists because of its charter with France—the police are French, its power supply comes from France. Do you think they're just going to say, 'Bonjour, Monsieur Spinola—welcome back'?"

"We're working on it," said Barry. "General Stemmer is here. He's working on a plan."

"Holy Catfish! You really are serious. But why?"

"Because they're going to throw me out of here!"

"Why would they want to do that?" Alec assumed Barry was suffering another bout of paranoia.

"It's a long story," groaned Barry. "It has something to do with a scoundrel I tried to help. He fed a ropy reporter a pack of lies about me and the people who run this place must have heard about it."

"So what?"

"So what? So what this!" Barry reached into his inside jacket pocket and thrust out his letter from the Bureau d'Etranger.

"They told me to shove off! And I don't know where else to go! And I only have 15 days left!"

Alec read the letter, whistled softly.

"I like it here," said Barry. "I want to stay. *And* I've always wanted my own country. This one will do—and it serves them right for trying to throw me out!"

"What the hell would you do with your own country?"

"Make my own laws and not be subject to anyone else's stupidity," barked Barry. "Laws are made to restrain individual freedom. I'm going to make a law that makes the making of laws *illegal*! Legalize drugs. Euthanasia will be legalized, too—freedom of choice—I'll, I'll . . . set an example to the world community. And people everywhere will sit up and take notice. My own passports won't restrict anyone from going anywhere. My currency will be based on the gold standard. And I'll outlaw lawyers! And bureaucrats. No bureaucrats. And taxes! No taxes! And anyone even suggesting taxes will be banished, along with all the lawyers and bureaucrats! That's what I'll do! And we'll treat criminals the old-fashioned way, with stockades. That'll keep crime down. And all policy decisions will be made by referendum only, and useful people get more votes than slouches, and politicians don't get paid. Did you know that in ancient Greece they didn't pay politicians?"

"I didn't." Alec sat impassively.

"It was an *honor* to serve. Not like the greedy buggers of today, taxing everyone up the wazoo while increasing their own salaries. Buggers, them all! My country will be a meritocracy. No Big Brother. No bureaucracy. I'll show everyone how to create utopia!"

"What about Spinola? Isn't Monaco suposed to be a principality, *Spinola's* principality, if you're successful?"

"Spinola's just a figurehead." Barry glanced furtively left and right. "*My* figurehead. We'll be a principality *and* a meritocracy."

"Spinola will be your puppet," said Alec.

"Exactly. We need a Spinola to spearhead the coup, justify it."

Alec shook his head from side to side. "I'm not sure you're going to find *this* Spinola very princely."

"The important thing is that his name is Spinola," said Barry. "That's all I care about. Are you in or out?"

"I don't know. This is bizarre, incredible. Are you sure you really want to do this?"

"I've been wanting to do something like this my whole life," said Barry. "It's a lifetime dream of mine to create my own country. And then, when I discovered the story of how the Grimaldis seized power in 1297, it hit me. The Spinolas have legitimate cause to re-claim Monaco as their own."

"You keep saying that," said Alec. "But 700 years is a long time. It has a tendency to legitimize a royal family no matter *how* they came to power. By your argument, the Indians have every right to take over the United States."

"They *do* and they *should*," huffed Barry. "The world is better served by a million tribes, communities, countries than the false borders we have now. Big countries lose touch with the people and become self-absorbed with power. I'm merely making my own contribution. Maybe, just maybe, if my plan works, the Indians will take note, others will take note, and we, the people, will take the world back from Big Brother. We'll be individuals again instead of numbers. Are you in or out?"

"Do I have to make up my mind this minute?" asked Alec.

"No. But by tonight. If you're not in, you can leave in the morning, and I'll pay you well for bringing Spinola over and to keep your confidence. If you're in, I will transfer *five hundred thousand dollars* into your account. You keep this whether the plan works or not. And if it works, you get *another five hundred thousand dollars*. A total of *one million dollars*. Plus you become Monaco's new chief of security at an annual salary of five hundred thousand dollars."

Alec said nothing. The money sounded damn good.

Maybe he could keep his role secret. He was good at that. Maybe, but don't count on it. What authority would prosecute him as an accomplice if the plan failed? Monaco? France? The United States? General Stemmer was key. What did *he* think about the whole operation?

"May I speak with J.J. before making a decision?"

"Of course," said Barry. "But I won't allow him to talk about operational details until you decide you're in. Now, when do I get to meet The Dentist?"

Alec checked his watch. It wasn't yet one o'clock. "How about 4:30? He ought to feel better by then."

"Fine. Not here. Let's meet at the American Bar in Hotel de Paris. It's empty at that time of the afternoon."

Alec walked back to Loews, his head buzzing with Barry's plan. A half million dollars! More money than an ex-government employee ever *dreamed* of. No more college problems. No more *any* problems. He returned to his room, took off his shoes, called room service and ordered a hamburger and a salad, which he enjoyed on his private terrace, then took a snooze.

When Alec next opened his eyes, it was a couple of minutes past four o'clock. Alec checked his watch. "Christ!" He rushed in and out of the shower and pulled on a suit. Then he knocked on Spinola's door. No answer. He knocked louder. Still no answer. He went back to his phone, called Spinola's room, and it rang and rang. The time was already 4:30. Alec cursed, went down to the lobby, checked the Café de la Mer and the piano bar. No Spinola.

Alec took the elevator back up to the sixth floor, looked around the outdoor pool—no Spinola—then left the hotel through the roof terrace exit. Barry was waiting, impatiently, when Alec walked into the American Bar at 4:45.

Barry's irritation at Alec's tardiness was compounded by the absence of Spinola. "You're late! Where's The Dentist?" he hissed, through clenched, crooked teeth etched in gold, trying to keep his anger from exploding through his mouth.

Alec held up his hands. "I can't find him. He's not in his room, not in the hotel. I'm going to kill him . . ."

"No you're not," snapped Barry. "He's the most crucial element of my plan. Just find him. Go find him. I'll call you at six sharp."

As Alec walked briskly back to Loews, it occurred to him where he was most likely to find the dentist. He didn't go to the house telephone nor to Spinola's room; Alec went straight to the Loews casino, a large, Las Vegas-style gaming room adjacent to the lobby.

Alec ziz-zagged the aisles of slots to reach the tables in back—roulette and craps. It was crowded, even at quarter-past five in the afternoon. Alec looked around as he walked, checking the bar, and stood there, taking it all in. Then he saw him, Spinola, at the far end of a craps table, shaking dice, getting ready to roll. "C'mon, gimme a nine, gimme a nine!" he heard Spinola shout.

Alec dashed over, stood behind Spinola as he rolled a seven. "Ah, shit!" said Spinola; the croupier scraped a mound of chips from the table. "Shit, shit, shit," Spinola's face twitched.

Alec tapped the dentist on the shoulder. Spinola turned.

"Oh, am I glad to see you," said Spinola. "I need that other five grand."

"Where the hell were you? We had a meeting with my client, remember?" Alec could see in Spinola's eyes that he'd already popped a few at the bar.

"Yeah, yeah, I was just about to come to your room. What time is it?"

"It's past five-thirty. The meeting was an hour ago."

"Acchhhh, must be the jet lag," said Spinola. "Now, about that other five grand . . ."

"Where are the traveller's checks I gave you?" asked Alec.

"Ummmm . . . they're gone."

"What do you mean, 'gone'."

"The forty-eight hundred. I lost it. I need the other five grand to win it back."

"You're a goddam moron!" Alec could no longer control himself.

"Don't call me that—or I'm outta here," said Spinola. "I didn't wanna come in the first place. You made me."

"All right, cool down," said Alec. "Let's go back to my room. My client is going to call at six, and then we're going to meet him. Okay?"

"Kapiche. Lemme just grab a drink . . ."

"No. We go to my room and wait. And do you think you could change into a suit?" Spinola was still wearing his plaid trousers and cream-colored sport coat, stained lightly with vomit.

They walked to the elevator, ascended to the fourth floor and Alec saw Spinola to his room. He stood outside and waited for the dentist to change. He wasn't taking any chances about losing his charge twice in one day. Spinola appeared ten minutes later in a three-piece, mauve-colored suit, 100 percent polyester from the shine of it, no tie and the same tired white loafers, now a shade of gray from the grit and rain of Hoboken. Spinola sported two gold chains beneath his open shirt, unbuttoned to his solar plexus.

"You call that a business suit?" asked Alec.

"Hey, do I criticize your choice of clothing?" said Spinola. "I can't help it if I have a flair for style."

Alec shook his head in disbelief. "Could you at least wear a tie? My client has a thing about ties."

"What thing?"

"He believes that in polite society a man always wears a tie in public. And he *has* paid for you to come here."

"I didn't bring one."

Alec rolled his eyes. "Okay, follow me. You can wear one of mine."

The pair went into Alec's room. Spinola made a beeline for the minibar and, while Alec pulled a tie from a drawer, the dentist quickly uncapped a mini-bottle of Glenfiddich scotch whiskey and mixed it with a bottle of Coca-Cola. "Cheers." Spinola raised his glass. "Care to join me?"

"I give up," said Alec. "How do you know my client doesn't want you to operate on him tonight?"

"So what if he does?"

"You're drinking."

"So what? It improves my technique!" Spinola laughed out loud, amused by his own wit, and farted loudly.

Alec tried not to notice, but had to hold his nose. "Here's a tie, put it on." It was a navy blue and burgundy striped tie, from Brooks Brothers.

"I can't wear this," said Spinola. "It'll spoil my image."

"Put it on," growled Alec.

Spinola put down his glass and begrudgingly buttoned his shirt and knotted the tie awkwardly beneath his floppy collar.

"I have this theory that ties cut off blood flow to the brain," said Spinola.

"Well, fortunately, we don't have to worry about that with you."

"Whattaya saying?" said Spinola. "Spell it out. I can leave right now, ya know?"

"Look," said Alec. "No more hassles. This is just a job for me. Let's get it over with and we can go our separate ways."

Spinola raised his glass. "I'll drink to that," he said, threw back the remaining half of his drink in one gulp and headed for the bar.

Alec went to block Spinola's way, but at that moment the telephone rang. Alec glanced at his watch, six o'clock, and he turned to answer the phone.

"Yes, Ted," said Alec. "I found him—he's here. Six-thirty? The *usual* place? Fine. We'll be there."

Spinola had already unsnapped another mini-bottle of Glenfiddich, poured himself a second scotch and coke. "Who's Ted?"

"My client."

"I thought his name was Barry?" He looked at Alec suspiciously.

"It is. He likes to be called Ted. His middle name is Theodore. Are you ready?"

"Yeah, lemme just finish this drink. Ya sure ya don't want one?"

"Yes, I'm sure."

Spinola knocked back his drink and Alec led him out.

They walked through a corridor connecting Loews roof terrace to Place du Casino. Spinola lit up when he saw the Grand Casino.

"Look, look!" Spinola pointed at the ornate Belle
Époque architecture. "The *Casino!* I'm going to be the
next guy to break the bank of Monte Carlo!"

Prophetic words, thought Alec, if Barry's plan actually works.

"Can't we just nip in for a look 'round?" asked Spinola.

"No, we cannot just nip in. We've already stood up
my client once today. And *you* couldn't just look around
a casino if your life depended on it, and in this case it
does, because if you disappear again I'll kill you."

They walked past the Café de Paris and around the
corner, quick left, right, and they brushed through the
revolving door into the Metropole lobby. It was completely empty.

Spinola immediately saw the bar adjacent to the lobby
and zipped inside, pursued hotly by Alec.

"We have to wait in the lobby," said Alec.

"I'm gettin' a drink," said Spinola.

Alec's attention was diverted by Barry Zubrick, who
appeared at the far end of the lobby. From a distance,
Barry looked to Spinola more like a homeless tramp in
Manhattan than a multi-millionaire resident of Monte
Carlo. Although it was near 60 degrees outside, Barry
wore a dark, baggy wool overcoat, and he carried a plastic shopping bag. The dentist looked at Alec with an
expression that said, Is this some kind of joke?

Alec made the introductions.

"Ted, this is The Dentist; Gerry, this is Ted."

Spinola reached out his hand. "Gerry Spinola, good
to meet ya."

"Shhhh!" Barry closed his eyes tight and banged his
right fist against his head. He turned to Alec. "Doesn't he
know not to use that name?"

"No," said Alec. "I think it's important *you* explain what's going on."

"Let's sit in the bar," said Barry. It was completely empty, except for a bartender preparing plates of nuts behind the bar.

"Damn good idea," said Spinola. "I could use a drink."

Barry chose a table as far away from the bartender as possible.

Spinola whipped a small flashlight from his pocket as Barry sat down. "Okay Ted, lemme take a quick peek inside those choppers."

"What?" snapped Barry.

"The abscess. Lemme take a peek, see what we're talking about here." Spinola tried to reach a finger into Barry's mouth, pry his lips apart.

"Stop it. Stop it!" screamed Barry. He flashed Alec a look of disgust. "Sit down!" he commanded Spinola. "I want to talk to you."

The bartender had waltzed over to see if anything was wrong. "Bon soir, monsieurs."

"Bone swar," said Spinola. "Gimme a large scotch and coke."

Alec ordered a dry martini, Bombay, straight up, olives.

Barry ordered Badoit, mineral water with a touch of fizz.

The barkeep returned to the bar.

"I don't have an abscess," said Barry. "And I didn't bring you over here for dental treatment."

Spinola froze for an instant, scared. If he were in Hoboken, a trap like this would mean he was about to be ground into pig meat.

"Do you remember," Barry continued, "answering an ad in the Wall Street Journal for a family reunion?"

"Yeah, yeah," said Spinola. "That was last week. How do you know about that?"

"That's why you're here," said Barry.

"You mean you brought me over here for a Spinola family reunion?" yelled Spinola.

"Shhhh, shhhhhh! Don't use the name 'Spinola'," whispered Barry.

Alec just sat back and closed his eyes. God knew where this was going.

"Why not?" asked Spinola. "That's my name."

"You," whispered Barry, "are a descendant of the man who rightfully owns Monaco. And it is my intention to give Monaco back to you and your family."

"What?" said Spinola.

"Your family owned Monaco up until 700 years ago. It was taken away by force from your ancestor by the Grimaldis"—Barry looked around, lowered his voice— "and we're going to take it back from the Grimaldis and put its rightful owner—you—in charge."

"And you, Ted, are nuts," said Spinola. "Where's my drink?"

The waiter reappeared, set out three drinks and returned to the bar.

"Do you want to rule Monaco?" asked Barry. "Historically, it belongs to you. Do you want it?"

Spinola took a large gulp of his drink and turned to Alec. "Is this guy for real?"

"I'm afraid so," replied Alec.

"Who rules Monaco now?" asked Spinola.

"The Grimaldi family," whispered Barry.

"And they want me to take over?"

"No," whispered Barry, a hint of exasperation in his voice. "They enjoy ruling Monaco. It has made them rich. Very rich."

"I don't get it," said Spinola. "So who's asking for the Spinolas to return?"

"Me," said Barry.

"Why?"

"So that you and me can rule this place together."

"And why should I share my birthright with you?" Spinola winked at Alec, who ignored the joke.

"Because without me," said Barry, "you go back to Hoboken and you don't get a million dollars a year for the rest of your life."

"A million dollars?" Spinola's eyes bulged.

"Each year, for life."

"What do I have to do?"

"Nothing," said Barry. "Just be available. And sign a treaty that grants me all territorial rights to the principality."

"So I don't get to rule?"

"No, you get a million a year. After the first year you don't even have to live in Monaco anymore."

"And how does it work? I'm supposed to show up, what-a they have, a castle or something?"

"A palace."

"I'm just supposed to show up at the palace, show 'em my passport, and they're gonna say, 'Gee, we've been waiting for you—we're outta here, it's all yours!' Is that it?"

"No," said Barry. "It's more complicated than that. We have to re-take Monaco the same way the Grimaldis took it from your ancestor: by force."

"Sounds dangerous," said Spinola.

"It's a gamble," said Barry.

Spinola liked the sound of that. He had a special affinity for the word *gamble*.

"The question is," continued Barry, "are you willing to take the gamble for a million a year?"

"The answer is," said Spinola. "I'm willing to take the gamble for *two* million a year, fifty grand up front, today. Another drink?" Spinola raised his empty glass.

Alec covered his eyes with his right hand. He could see it coming.

"Now see here," barked Barry. "My terms are fair. You are taking advantage of my generosity."

"And you," said Spinola, "are trying to take advantage of my good name."

Alec laughed. Spinola signaled the bartender, who strode over.

"Another scotch and cola, gar-sone," said Spinola. "Anything for youz guys?"

Barry said nothing, bristling, waiting for the bartender to disappear.

"We'll make it a million and a half a year," huffed Barry.

Spinola burped. "Whatta 'bout up front?"

"The money depends on success," said Barry.

"Nah," said Spinola. "I gotta have somethin' up front. Good faith. Fifty grand's worth-a good faith."

"Twenty thousand," said Barry, "against the first million."

"You got a deal," said Spinola, thrusting out his palm. "Plus the five grand you still owe me."

"What five grand?"

"Half of the ten, my payment for coming out here, 'member?"

"Okay, okay," snapped Barry. He reached into his inside pocket and pulled from it a folded document. "This is a little agreement I put together. It says in writing what I've already told you: that you agree in principle to grant me territorial rights to Monaco in consideration of a fee, which I'll change to reflect our agreed price." Barry altered the figure of one million dollars to one million, five hundred thousand with his pen and initialed the change, and held the document out to Spinola. "For your signature," said Barry.

Spinola read through the one-page agreement. "You still gotta add the up-front moulah."

Barry snatched back the paper, and with his pen wrote: "Advance of $30,000 to be paid upon execution of this agreement."

"Okay," said Barry. "You got what you wanted. Sign."

"I don't sign nuthin' without checking with Vinnie," said Spinola.

"Who the hell is Vinnie?" Barry threw up his arms.

"He's my cousin," said Spinola. "A paralegal in Jersey City. Can we fax it to him?"

"Of course we can't fax it to him!" Barry blew a gasket, looked around, lowered his voice. "They bug the phones here, faxes, too. You want the whole world to know what we're doing?"

"I can't sign this without Vinnie. He takes care of all my legal matters."

"What's wrong with you!" hollered Barry. "There's no small print, nothing—only a simple statement that says in writing what we just talked about!"

"Doesn't matter. I gotta keep this hid from my second wife. Vinnie knows how to do that."

"I've never heard such nonsense," snapped Barry. "If you don't sign right now, the deal's off!"

"Okay by me," Spinola rose. "I think it's a crazy idea anyway."

"Wait a minute, wait a minute.," Barry flapped his right hand. "Sit down. Let's talk about it."

"There's nuthin' to talk about," said Spinola. "I don't sign nuthin' without Vinnie."

"What about a lawyer here?" asked Barry. "I know a lawyer you could use." But as he said it, Barry knew damn well he wasn't about to let Alan Bennett in on his plan.

"Nah, it's gotta be Vinnie. If I can't fax it, I'll fly back and show it to him."

"No way," said Barry. "There's only one copy of this agreement and it stays with me."

"If the agreement can't go to Vinnie," said Spinola, "let's bring Vinnie to the agreement. But he'd probably wanna be paid."

"It comes out of your advance," said Barry.

"Nah," said Spinola. "You pay."

"Look," said Barry, all indignance. "When I want legal advice, I pay for it. If *you* want legal advice, *you* pay for it."

"I'd pay for a fax," said Spinola. "But youz the one sayin' I can't."

"Okay, okay, I get the point. I'll pay his expenses to get here, economy, and one night in a hotel. But you cover his fee."

"Done." Spinola drained his drink. "Gar-sone!" Spinola waved to the bartender. "Fill 'er up!"

*****

The Vista Palace Hotel, perched precariously on a mountainside high above Cap Martin, possessed the most spectacular view to be had of Monaco. Its twelve-foot floor-to-ceiling windows afforded panoramic views of the Riviera stretching from the Tete de Chien, a majestic alp behind the principality, to Italy.

Barry Zubrick, Alec Perry and General J. J. Stemmer sat in the Vista Palace Hotel bar, studying a lit-up, nighttime Monaco post-card sprawled out before them.

Earlier, Alec had returned to Loews with Spinola to call Vinnie; Spinola's cousin agreed to fly out the following evening, and Alec left Spinola in his room where the dentist promised to stay put; order room service and have an early night to beat jet lag.

About 10:30, after snacking in the Café de la Mer, Alec walked to the taxi rank near the Hotel de Paris and took a cab up the mountain to the Vista Palace. He could have nailed a taxi outside Loews, but the time had come to exert caution in his movements, and this came second nature to Alec when the need arose.

Barry had also arrived by taxi; J.J., by car, rented at Nice airport.

The three men sat in a far corner, next to the window, where the hotel was supported on stilts. J.J. was a stocky five-foot-five and nearly bald—with a big cigar, which he never lit, just held, and occasionally chomped.

"This hotel," said J.J., "will be operational headquarters. I've booked the whole place for a 'weekend convention' and this is where my men will stay. It is a perfect vantage point and logistically sound."

"I'd like to go on," continued the general, looking Alec square in the face. "Barry says you haven't decided yet. Are you in, Alec?"

Alec looked back into the general's eyes. "J.J., is this going to work?"

"Piece of cake," said the general. "I can take Monaco easy, no problem, few casualties, if any. That's my primary role in this operation and it'll work."

"The problem, as I see it," said Alec, "is France."

"Exactly," said the general. "The success or failure of the overall op boils down to France. We'll be in control of Monaco before a single cop can fart. But, unless persuaded otherwise, there isn't a doubt in hell, France will respond militarily in the aftermath. It is their *role* to protect the Grimaldi reign—they are pledged to do that."

"So how . . . ?"

"You know the French, Alec," The general puffed on his unlit cigar. "They're very open-minded about secret deals—you're privy to how they've dealt with the Palestinians and Shiites all these years. We have to deal with them, make it worth their while to go along. The French are always willing to deal if their self-interests are served."

"And what role do you have in mind for me?" asked Alec.

"Right now, your role is purely recon and intelligence. A vital element of dealing with France will be the legitimacy of our claim. We'll need you to study Monaco's constitution, its form of government, its history and make the best case we can for a Spinola rule. We'll want to prepare a report, justifying our action, and disseminate it to the media and the UN at the end of Phase One, the taking of Monaco."

Alec nodded. Stemmer's authority was assuring, far more assuring than Barry Zubrick's eccentricities.

"You would establish a cover as a freelance writer,"

said the general. "Say you're researching a book on Monaco, a novel, whatever."

"My hesitation," said Alec, "is Spinola. He's a clown."

"Just as well," Barry cut in. "It'll be easier for me to take control."

"As far as I'm concerned, Alec, he's just a name," said J.J., "and it'll be *your* role to keep him in line."

"And another part of your assignment," added Barry, "will be to study SBM, the Society Bains de la Mer, which is virtually Monaco, Incorporated. SBM is a publicly traded company, controlled by the Grimaldi family, and it owns all the casinos in Monaco and all the biggest hotels. The question will be, what is the best way to seize control of SBM from the Grimaldis. Is the controlling interest owned by them personally, or does it belong to the government? In a worst case scenario, we could *nationalize* SBM, but we risk isolating its other shareholders and we want to create the image that Monaco is a wonderful place to do business, not the other way around."

"So the real question is," said the general. "Are you with us?"

Alec gazed out the window, down to Monaco below, so inviting, so magical—one could be nothing but tantalized by its sheer beauty, near perfection.

"What's the downside, J.J.?" asked Alec.

"If France can't be 'persuaded,' and if they get their hands on us, they'll probably give us to the French Foreign Legion for target practice."

"Why are you doing it, J.J.?" asked Alec.

"For the same reason mountain climbers climb mountains, I suppose," said the general. "I'm a soldier. *And* I need the money." He laughed heartily. "Even a retired general can't keep up with the cost of living these days."

Alec drained his glass, stood up to look down the coastline to Menton, and Italy beyond, its peninsular jutting into he sea so gently, soft curves dancing with the silky blue sea.

"Gentlemen, I'm in," said Alec. "Though I must point out that a plan is only as strong as its weakest link, and our weak link is that damn dentist. Are you sure we can't find another Spinola?"

"There's no time," said J.J. "And *this* Spinola already knows what we're planning. One week from tomorrow night, on Easter eve, we make our move. The Grimaldis traditionally spend Easter weekend at Roc Agel, their country retreat in the mountains. It is a busy holiday weekend, the principality will be packed with Italian tourists. And with so many thousands of people concentrated in so small an area, France won't be rash. The French will be forced to give our occupation the reasoned, measured response we need from them."

6

Alec was up early the next morning. He'd slept probably four hours a night for the previous two nights; jet lag—plus the scope of the operation of which he was now a conspirator.

It was sunny and quiet as Alec strolled outside Loews, to the Café de Paris for a cappucino and croissant in the open-air. He watched stylishly-dressed Frenchmen with their leather handbags walk to work. What a tranquil life it was in this bubble of paradise. You could spend the whole day sitting in cafés and not feel pressured to *do* something; not be burdened by the American work ethic. It sure was different in Bethesda, Alec mused. Even though he was unemployed, Alec felt guilty if he didn't have a daily schedule of chores and assignments. But here in Monaco, it seemed the most natural thing in the world to sit back, sip cappucino, watch the world pass before him— and feel great about it.

When the kiosk inside the Café de Paris' shopping arcade opened, Alec bought an *International Herald Tribune* and read it from cover to cover over a second cappucino. The *Tribune* had a way of compacting the world's most important news into a manageable format, devoid of full-page ads and discount coupons. Even the classified ads were interesting.

A very civilized way to live one's life.

At 8:30, Alec walked back to Loews and stopped at the concierge's desk to inquire about schools in the area that taught French.

"There are two," said the concierge. "Both very good. One is in Villefranche, about 12 kilometers from here. The other is in Cap d'Ail, walking distance." The concierge looked up both in the telephone directory and scribbled their numbers on a notepad, tore the sheet from its binding and handed it to Alec.

Alec returned to his room and touch-keyed the Institut de Française in Cap d'Ail.

"Bonjour, madame. Parlez vous Anglais?" asked Alec.

"Oui, monsieur. Can I help you?"

"I hope so. I am staying in Monaco, doing research, and I need a translator to translate from French to English. Do you have anyone on your teaching staff available to do this part-time?"

"The teachers are very busy, but there is a woman in administration who may be interested. She's not here now, but if you give me your number I'll ask her to call you later this morning. Her name is Isabelle."

Alec gave her his details, then sat on his balcony overlooking the sea, reclining in a deck chair. The ringing telephone jolted him from a doze about an hour later.

"Hello? This is Isabelle, from the Institut de Française."

"Yes, bonjour," said Alec. "Thanks for calling back. I am doing research here in Monaco and I need help translating from French to English. Is this something that might interest you?"

"Yes, I could," said Isabelle. "What kind of translation?"

"I need information on Monaco's history. I'm hoping you can help me find books as well as translate for me."

"I think so. I was worried that you wanted technical translating. I'm no good with that."

"No, no, nothing technical," said Alec. "Simple subjects—history, government. Would you like to meet to discuss it?"

"Yes, but it would have to be at night. I work all day in this job."

"Would tonight be okay?"

"Yes. I usually finish here at seven. Can we meet at 7:30?"

"Only if you let me buy you dinner," said Alec. "Do you have a favorite restaurant?"

"Let's meet at Le Texan," said Isabelle.

"Where is Le Texan?"

"In the Condamine quarter, near the port. I don't know the address, but your concierge will know."

Alec would have called the other school, in Villefranche, but he liked the sound of Isabelle, liked her accent.

Alec didn't see Spinola all day; didn't want to see Spinola, and he assumed the dentist was sleeping off jet lag and booze. He hoped Spinola was staying out of the casino. At six, Alec left Loews and wandered down the hill to La Condamine, the port district. It was so unlike Monte Carlo—down to earth, not touristy, and it bustled with food stores and corner bistros. He strolled the wide promenade along the port, walked up Rue Princesse Caroline, a pedestrian precinct and La Condamine's main shopping street. At the top, it intersected with Rue Grimaldi, an artery for traffic. Alec wondered if crazy old Barry Zubrick had a mind to change all the street names. Rue Spinola and Avenue Zubrick. Maybe even Boulevard Perry. Alec walked left onto Rue Grimaldi, then made a right up Avenue Prince Pierre to Monaco's train station. It was busy. The hundreds of Italians who worked in Monaco by day were commuting home to Ventimighlia and San Remo. Alec cut down a set of stairs opposite the station to Rue Turbie, a narrow, winding street, and came out in front of Hotel de France. He walked over to inspect its rate card, plastered to the window. A single room without bath was priced at 150 francs. Even with a weak dollar, it converted to 25 bucks a night! Who said you had to be a millionaire to live in Monaco?

Alec followed Rue Turbie back to Rue Grimaldi, inspecting the tiny shops. Bally Shoes. A pen shop. A picture window crammed full with Western-style belts and boots. Breitling watches. It was so different from Monte Carlo, occupied by only the most exclusive names, Cartier, Vuitton, Hermes . . . .

As Rue Grimaldi rounded a bend, Alec saw the sign "Avenue Suffren Reymond," and he knew Le Texan was near. He walked ten steps and suddenly realized he was standing smack in front of the glassed-in terrace of the Tex-Mex restaurant. It was only 7:15, early by French standards, but Le Texan was doing brisk business. Alec entered the terrace and then another door to the inner restaurant. The long Alamo bar was busy, and down the far end he noticed a pretty girl with long brown hair, on her own, looking at him quizzically. He *knew* it was Isabelle. She'd beat him at his own trick, arriving early. Alec walked down the bar, and when he got close to her, mouthed, "Isabelle?"

"Yes." Isabelle was sipping on a margarita. "You must be Alec. I finished early today."

"Shall we sit down?"

Alec nabbed a small table for two across from the bar. Isabelle gazed across the table at Alec, expectantly, and he began by asking questions about her. Where was she from? Paris. How long had she been at the institut in Cap d'Ail. Three years. What did she think of Monaco? "I go to Nice for fun". How old was she? Twenty-six. And, all along, her big brown eyes looking directly into his. She liked Americans, she said. She had been to the States the previous summer, drove cross-country, loved the experience, wanted to return soon.

And then it was Isabelle's turn. "What kind of translating do you need me to do?"

"I'd like to find out as much as possible about Monaco's history, about its system of government," said Alec. "I assume there are books on the subject, and I'm hoping you can help me find them. I also assume they'll be in French, and that's why I need a translator."

"How long are you here?" asked Isabelle.

Alec loved the way she spoke, in fluid English, but with a marvelous French accent. "A few weeks. I need to get started as soon as possible."

"I could go to the bookstores tomorrow in my lunch hour," said Isabelle, "see what there is."

Alec pulled a 500 franc note from his pocket. "Use this to buy whatever books you find." He couldn't stop looking into Isabelle's eyes; they seemed to be studying him, consuming him. It was funny how French women could be so, so *sensual* with just a look.

Alec's highly-focused attention was suddenly cut short by the high-pitched sound of his name across the bar.

"Alllec!"

Alec looked up and saw Gerry Spinola down the bar, waving at him, guzzling from a bottle of Corona beer.

"Alec, how'd *you* find this place?" Spinola snaked over and pulled a chair up to the small table. "Gerry Spinola, Glad ta meet ya," he said to Isabelle, thrusting out a hand. "Where ya been hidin' *her*?"

"This is Isabelle," said Alec. "We just met. Isabelle is going to do some translating for me."

Spinola winked and punched Alec lightly on the shoulder. "Yeah, yeah. I like the sound of *that*."

"What are you doing here?" said Alec.

"I heard this is the hottest bar in town. *And* they speak English, can you beat that?" Spinola leaned over and whispered in Alec's ears. "Can you believe these broads?" He gestured down the bar—all the women were model material. "It's those short black skirts and black stockings that drive me nuts!" He looked back up, at Isabelle. "French women are so different from American women."

"What difference?" asked Isabelle.

"They're *happy* to be women," said Spinola. "Most of the women in the United States want to be men, the way they dress, the way they talk." He took a swig of beer. "Vinnie's coming in tomorrow," he said to Alec. "Ya wanna fetch him with me?"

"What time?"

"Whattaya mean? Same Delta flight we came in on yesterday, 'bout ten a.m."

"Okay. Ask the concierge to book a taxi for nine."

Spinola leaned over for more whispering. "I'm outta dough, Alec. Ya got some to tie me over?"

Alec blinked heavily, reached into his trouser pocket and pulled a 500 franc note from his pocket.

"Ahh, c'mon," whispered Spinola, "that don't buy doodly-squat in this town."

Alec pulled another 500 franc note from his pocket.

Spinola grabbed the banknotes. "Pleasure ta meet ya, Isabella." Then to Alec, "I'll be at the bar if ya need me."

Not likely.

"Who was that funny man," asked Isabelle.

Here goes. Spinola was already complicating things.

"Someone I met at Loews, sitting out on the pool terrace."

"Why did you give him money?"

"Uhhh, he had some bad luck at the casino. He's expecting a money wire from the States and he'll pay me back."

The pair ordered, ate fajitas and talked about the States as Le Texan bustled around them.

"Look, there's Princess Stephanie." Isabelle pointed to a table in a far corner behind Alec. The princess was with friends, drinking margaritas, laughing.

"This is one of the few places for young people to have fun in Monaco," said Isabelle. "And, usually, when a place becomes too much fun in Monaco, the police close it down."

"Why?"

"Because the older people complain. They don't like noise. Monaco tries to always please its wealthy, retired community."

"Then how come this place gets away with it?"

"See that lady over there?" Isabelle pointed to a redhead, an older version of Jane Fonda, sitting on the terrace, sipping red wine and chatting with two men. "She's the owner, American. *And* she was Princess Grace's best friend. That's how things work around here."

"You don't seem to like Monaco very much," said Alec.

"It's small-minded. And too controlled. I prefer Nice. It's a big city. You can get lost in it."

Alec loved the way she said that. He wanted to get lost with Isabelle in Nice.

Gerry Spinola was still standing at the bar, into his fifth beer, when Alec and Isabelle left. He waved at Alec and blew a kiss at Isabelle, then returned his attention to the ladies lined up along the bar.

Alec walked Isabelle to her Peugeot, parked around the corner.

"Can I drop you at your hotel?" asked Isabelle.

"No, thank you. I enjoy the walk. I don't walk enough back home—our culture is based around cars."

"I'll call you after I've been to the bookstores," said Isabelle. "Maybe we could meet tomorrow night?"

"I'd like that very much."

It wasn't the margaritas that made Alec warm and tingly and lightheaded as he walked along the harbor. It was the image of Isabelle; her brown eyes, her accent.

The almost full moon shone brightly onto the large yachts, bobbing gently upon the water. As Alec walked out toward the jetty, he looked back at La Condamine, glowing golden in the night. Alec followed a sign to the *ascenseur* and was awed by the sheer elegance and elaborate security that went into a simple elevator. The long passageway was marble and brass, and there wasn't a square inch of hall and foyer not monitored by one of three moving cameras, all connected, Alec supposed, to police headquarters. It felt eerie. Alec knew he was being watched. This was the price residents of Monaco paid for its crime-free reputation. The elevator itself was monitored by a camera mounted in its ceiling, and when the elevator opened, its passengers were greeted with yet another bank of cameras.

Alec whistled softly as he walked along the terrace between the Grand Casino the Loews roof terrace. The night air made him sleepy, and though Alec attempted to watch CNN, he was sound asleep within two minutes of hitting a pillow.

Alec arose at 7:30, as the Mediterranean light filled his room. He repeated his procedure of a morning earlier—Café de Paris, the *Herald Tribune*—a decidedly delightful way to start the day.

At 8:50 he knocked on Gerry Spinola's door. There was no answer. He rapped again, loudly.

"Go away!" hollered a muffled voice from inside.

Alec knocked again. "It's me, Alec. Get up!"

A minute later Spinola's unsteady figure opened the door about a foot. He was hunched over, eyes bloodshot and puffy, skin a pallid green. "Whatta-ya doing here so early," Spinola's voice was the texture of gravel.

"Have you forgotten your cousin Vinnie?"

"Oh, shit." Spinola covered his eyes. "What time is it?"

"A few minutes before nine. The taxi is waiting."

"Oh, shit. Can you go without me?"

"Go to hell." Alec started to walk away.

"Wait a second, wait a second. Don't go. I'll get dressed."

"I'll be in the lobby," said Alec. "If you're not down in 15 minutes, I'm history."

"Okay, okay." Spinola closed the door.

The dentist appeared soon after in his multi-color plaid trousers and a sickly expression.

"I hope you're not going to puke again," said Alec. "Tell me right now so I can split."

"Nah, I'm okay. Damn spic beer—does it every time."

The taxi whizzed the pair to Nice-Côte d'Azur airport on the auto route, behind the mountains, and though it was relatively free of dramatic curves, it was fast, the driver pushing 120 kilometers an hour. The plane had already landed when they arrived, but its passengers had not yet passed through Immigration.

Spinola grabbed a fast expresso at a coffee counter as passengers from Delta's flight 82 began to appear. They kept coming and coming.

"Spinneeeeeeee!"

Spinola froze. The shrill voice came from a heavily made-up blond dressed in red leather, just outside the Immigration booth.

"Spinneeeeeeeeeee!" The blond dropped her bags and ran to Spinola, jumping uninvited into his arms.

"Vicky, whatta you doin' here?" Spinola scratched his head.

"Vinnie brought me with him. Oh, I'm sooo excited—the Coat Dah Sure! Spinny, why didn't you tell me you was here?"

Vinnie scooped up Vicky's toiletry case and carryall and caught up with the threesome. Alec was standing a few steps back, horrified.

"Eh, Spinny," said Vinnie. "Whattaya think of this, huh?" Vinnie looked no better than he had three days earlier when he'd driven Alec and Spinola to JFK. Unshaven, baggy trousers, fly unzipped. "Vic wouldn't let me go without her. And they had a special two-for-the-price-of-one deal, ya know, take a squeeze for free."

"Oh, Spinnny," cooed Vicky, not letting go of the

haggard-looking dentist. "You and me—in *France!*—ain't it romantic?"

"Yeah, yeah, Vic." Spinola was unable to conceal his lack of enthusiasm. "What a surprise."

"I wanna go shoppin'. Can we go shoppin'?" asked Vicky.

"Yeah, yeah, sure," said Spinola. "But let's go back to the hotel first. I could use a nap."

"Oh, Spinnny, you're sooo romantic."

Alec was sorry he had come to the airport. Was sorry he had come to Monaco. What had begun as a simple clown act was turning into a three-ring circus. But then he thought of Isabelle. He would see her tonight. And the warmth of her image sustained him.

Vinnie and Vicky collected their luggage—Vicky had four large cases.

"Jeez," said Spinola, "How long you planning to stay, Vic?"

"As long as you want me, honey-pie."

Vinnie looked around, scratched his crotch. "Let's boogie."

Out at the taxi rank, a cab driver squeezed Vicky's luggage into a Mercedes station wagon, and they were off, along the Basse Corniche, the coastal route. Every few minutes Vicky would squeal, "Oh, look at that! Look at that! I can't believe it—the Coat Dah Sure! What'll my friends say? Spinny, can we stop and get some postcards?"

"Don't worry Vic," said Spinola. "There're plenty at the hotel."

Alec, in the front seat, leaned back and closed his eyes; tried to block out the commotion behind him. He thought about Isabelle's big brown eyes, how they had studied him the night before.

Vinnie opened his eyes. "So, whatta youz guys need my expertise for?"

"Later," said Spinola. "It's a secret."

"Oh, Spinneeeee," cooed Vicky. "You mean like you're a spy or something?".

"Yeah, yeah. Somethin' like that."

Alec flashed Spinola a look of disgust from the front seat.

"Oh, that's sooo romantic," said Vicky. "We're gonna have *fun* here."

Vinnie burped and leaned back in his seat, head against the window, eyes closed, and Vicky continued to squeal with excitement.

Arriving at Loews, Alec pulled Spinola off to the side while Vinnie filled out a registration card and Vicky studied the jewelry on display at Fred the Jewelers.

"You've got to get rid of her," Alec whispered.

"You think I want her here?"

"That's not the issue," said Alec. "She's got to go."

"Yeah, yeah—I'll send her home with Vinnie."

"I'm going out." said Alec. "Tell Vinnie we're going to meet our client—don't say his name—at 4:30. Meet me down here in the lobby at four sharp. Got it?"

"Yeah, yeah."

It was close to noon. Alec walked past the shops inside Loews to Café de la Mer and ordered lunch, then returned to his room, reclined on the balcony and napped in the afternoon sun, awaiting Isabelle's call.

The phone rang just past 2:30.

"I've got the books you need," said Isabelle. "I found them at Quartier Latin, a bookstore in Monte Carlo that stocks textbooks for schoolchildren in Monaco."

"Great. Can we meet tonight?"

"Yes, but let's go somewhere out of Monaco. I'll pick you up at 7:30, okay?"

"Perfect," said Alec. "I'll be in the lobby, watching for you."

Alec touch-keyed Barclay's Bank and asked if a wire transfer had been received.

"Oui, Monsieur Perry. Four hundred thousand ECUs."

Alec smiled in appreciation of Barry Zubrick's efficiency.

*****

Barry Zubrick gazed at yet another fax from Gary Lincoln, the fifth in as many days. This latest missile, the most threatening of all, issued an ultimatum: deal with me or I'll tell all to the *Herald*.

Bill Blade pestered Lincoln relentlessly after his exposé appeared; he even showed up at Lincoln's Melbourne office with a photographer and ambushed Lincoln when he left his office for lunch.

Blade wanted an in-person interview; Lincoln wanted Blade off his back. He also wanted an immediate wire transfer from Barry to pay for a three-week vacation in Europe. Not only would he be able to get away from Blade—Lincoln stated in his fax to Barry—but this would enable Lincoln to visit Monaco and "hash everything out" with Barry "in person."

If such funds were not received within 72 hours, Lincoln continued, he would have no choice but to sit down with Blade and relieve himself of "all the sordid details about our relationship."

Barry knew deep down that Lincoln's faxes, his threats, were best left ignored, but Barry could not contain the bile that rose within him. He possessed a streak of indignation that never quit, and when provoked, he could not resist a good fax fight.

And so Barry composed the following fax to Gary Lincoln:

> There is 0 to 'hash out' and I don't want to see yor ugly face. U will not now, not ever, get another $ from me. Becuz U R a thief, a liar, scum. U hav no shame. I want no more to do with U. Don't fax me again. Get out of my life. If U say slanderous lies about me, U will hear from my lawyers pronto.
>
> BZ

Barry fed the message into his fax machine, pressed Gary Lincoln's number and hit the start button.

*****

Alec expected the worst as he descended to the lobby. But there they were, Spinola and Vinnie, standing near the front entrance to Loews at four on the dot, looking like a pair of low-budget tourists. The dentist was wearing his three-piece mauve suit *and* Alec's tie, and Vinnie was dressed in an ill-fitting check sport coat and dark slacks slipping beneath a pot belly, cuffs dragging on the floor over his heavy shoes, no tie, chewing on a toothpick. Alec looked around, and was relieved to see Vicky nowhere in sight.

"She's at the pool," Spinola offered.

"Okay guys, follow me," commanded Alec, and he led the way up Avenue Speluges to the Galerie Metropole, up the escalators to the Metropole Hotel lobby.

Vinnie looked around, took in the frescoes and the chandeliers and crystal candelabras and whistled. "Sure beats Hoboken."

"No drinks," said Alec firmly, "until business is complete."

They sat down on one of the smooth, red velvety sofas and waited quietly. Barry Zubrick appeared through the revolving door a few minutes later, looked over his shoulder, and shuffled over to where Alec was sitting.

"This is Ted," Alec said to Vinnie. "Ted, this is Vinnie."

Vinnie stuck out his hand. Barry hesitated, offered his hand for a quick shake, then quickly brushed his fingers on the seat of his trousers. God, how he hated meeting new people, if only because they always wanted to shake hands.

Spinola spoke. "Ted has a business proposition, Vin, and . . ."

"Wait," said Alec, holding up a hand. "Let *me* explain." He turned to face Vinnie. "Ted has prepared a short agreement for Gerry to sign. Gerry wanted you to read it first because you are a paralegal."

Vinnie nodded solemnly, an expression of self-importance on his freshly shaven face. Alec gently took the one-page document from Barry and handed it to Vinnie.

Vinnie read slowly, and as he neared the end he blew a long-winded whistle.

"Holy shit," said Vinnie. "Is this for real?"

"It is," snapped Barry impatiently.

Vinnie turned to Spinola. "You wanna do this?"

"Why not?"

Vinnie shrugged. "Looks dangerous. Are you sure these guys know what they's doin'?"

"Who cares?" said Spinola. "Look at the up-front dough."

Vinnie read the agreement a second time, then looked up. "What's my cut?"

"Huh?" said Spinola.

"What's my cut?"

"For what?"

"For coming all the way out here and giving you my full professional service."

"Whatta you talking about? You're my cousin. I'm paying your way to come out here and paying you a grand for your advice. Period."

"I wanna cut," said Vinnie.

"What kinda cut?"

"Fifteen percent."

"Whatta you, crazy?" Spinola reached over and slapped Vinnie across the face.

Vinnie rose, red-faced. "Why you sonofabitch, I'll kill you for that!"

Vinnie grabbed Spinola by the tie and the two men clenched fists as Alec jumped up to intercede, pushing Vinnie back into his chair and holding Spinola at bay.

The valet from outside rushed through the revolving door and was joined by a bellhop to see what the commotion was about. Barry grabbed the agreement from the table and sprinted out the back way. He was gone.

"It's okay, it's okay," Alec assured the hotel employees. Then to Spinola and Vinnie, "You stupid jerks, sit down and behave yourselves."

The two cousins didn't really want to fight. They looked at each other with contemptuous expressions and sat down.

"It might be all right to act like this in Hoboken,"

hissed Alec. "But you *will not* act like this in Monaco. Understood?"

"He started it," said Vinnie, glowering at his cousin.

"You guinea shit," scowled Spinola. "You deserved it."

"You're calling *me* a guinea shit?" said Vinnie. "*You're* a guinea shit!"

"Cool it!" Alec commanded. "You're *both* acting like guinea shits. Let's figure this out calmly."

"There ain't nuttin' to figure," said Vinnie. "I wanna cut."

"Why should *you* getta cut?" asked Spinola.

"It's my family, too, for chrissakes!"

"Whatta ya talkin' about? You're an Esposito."

"My *mother* was a Spinola!" shouted Vinnie.

"Keep quiet!" hissed Alec. An assistant manager had already rounded the corner, and was watching them from a distance.

Vinnie looked at Alec. "My mother and his father were sister and brother. I have as much right to this deal as him. And all I'm asking is a measly 15 percent."

Alec looked at Spinola. "You know, it was *your* idea to bring your cousin here."

"I didn't know he was such a thieving bastard," said Spinola.

"Oh, you calling me a *bastard* now?" yelled Vinnie. "You sayin' I'm not a Spinola, that my mother was a whore?" He jumped up and hit Spinola with a punch to the jaw and knocked the dentist out of his chair, onto the floor.

Alec rose, scooped Spinola off the floor and quickly marched him through the revolving door, leaving Vinnie behind. "Your mother was a whore!" shouted Vinnie, waving his fist. "I'm more Spinola than you are!"

Alec hustled Spinola back to Loews. The last thing he wanted was for police to be called, start questioning the dentist and his cousin. That would be the end of everything.

"That fucking animal broke my tooth." Spinola probed his mouth with a finger.

"Good thing you're a dentist," said Alec.

"I don't want nuthin' more to do with him," said Spinola.

"Does that mean you're ready to sign?"

"Yeah, yeah. Where's the agreement?"

"Ted ran off with it. We'll have to see him later. Right now I want you to stay in your room, order room service for dinner, *don't* go out. I'll take care of Vinnie."

Alec walked back up to the Metropole, found Vinnie in the bar and sat down at his table, opposite him.

Vinnie was sullen, nursing a Jack Daniel's on the rocks.

"You're leaving tomorrow morning, Delta flight 83." Alec was matter of fact.

Vinnie's eyes narrowed, glowering. "Who says?"

In a nano-second, Alec's right hand gripped Vinnie's adam's apple. Vinnie made low-pitched gurgling noises; his face furned purple.

"*I'm* saying." Alec released his grip.

Vinnie rubbed his neck and coughed.

"You will be paid two thousand dollars for coming here," said Alec. "And you're lucky I'm feeling generous. If you're not on tomorrow's flight, you'll get nothing. And if one word of this gets out—here or in New Jersey— I'll personally hunt you down and cut your balls off. Kapiche?"

Vinnie nodded, still rubbing his adam's apple.

* * * * *

Alec's phone was ringing as he entered his room at Loews. It was Barry Zubrick.

"What's going on? Where's The Dentist?" Barry was agitated.

"It's under control," said Alec.

"Under control? You call that ruckus under control?" hollered Barry. "They may have ruined everything!"

"Calm down. I'm handling it the best I can. It's under control. The Dentist is ready to sign."

"And what about that, that beast, the cousin?"

"He's out of the picture."

"I'm not going out again today," said Barry. "Too dangerous. I'm sure the cops already know."

"That's fine," said Alec. "The Dentist is in his room. He's staying put. We'll re-group in the morning."

If it weren't for Isabelle, thought Alec, *he'd* be on tomorrow's flight, too.

Alec showered, changed from his suit into blazer and khakis, and parked himself downstairs in the piano bar over a dry martini, waiting for Isabelle.

At 7:30, Alec stood near the sliding glass entrance. Isabelle's pale blue Peugeot rounded into Loews' forecourt. She leaned over, unlocked the passenger-side door. Isabelle looked more beautiful than he had remembered her. As she drove off, Isabelle reached behind to the back seat and grabbed a plastic carrier bag, which she handed to Alec.

Alec looked puzzled, then remembered the reason for their meeting. "Oh, the books—great!" He pulled two red, cloth-bound books from the bag. They were in French, companion volumes by Jean Pastorelli.

"These are the best books on Monaco," said Isabelle. "I hope they are what you wanted."

Alec skimmed through the books. They seemed to cover everything.

"They're perfect, you've done well. Where are we going?"

Isabelle swung the car down to Avenue Princesse Grace, along the public beach, and across the border into France, then up, up, several hairpin turns, into the mountain. "Rocquebrune Village," said Isabelle.

They drove silently as Alec perused the two volumes a second time. He looked up as they passed the Vista Palace Hotel, then put the books back inside the bag to enjoy the panoramic views.

"It is so beautiful here," said Alec. "You are fortunate to live in such a beautiful part of the world. Do you plan to stay?"

"Yes, I love it here."

"Don't you miss Paris?" Alec had fond recollections of the two years he had been stationed in Paris.

"A little. My mother is still there, and I like to visit her. But I don't want to live in Paris anymore."

"Why not?"

"It's too busy, too crowded and cold. I like it better here."

Isabelle made a sharp left turn into a narrow road, and up a steep incline. "This is Rocquebrune." She swung into a lot and parked. "You can't drive in the Village—we have to walk the rest of the way."

Another steep hill deposited them into a village hub, a wide terrace with a view of Monaco in the distance, a café and a quaint inn called Les Deux Frères. They stood, watching a train below, clinging to the coastline en route to Monaco beneath a star-filled sky.

"This is heaven," said Alec.

"Come, let's see the Village." Isabelle touched Alec's elbow. He loved her touch.

Isabelle led Alec into the maze of narrow, winding brick and cobblestoned paths, unlevel, up and down—a medieval village, untouched by architects for many centuries.

"All the tourists go to Eze Village, and that's why I like Rocquebrune. It's not at all commercial—just a simple village. You see that castle up there?" Isabelle pointed to a chateau with a flag fluttering overhead, at the village's highest level.

Alec nodded.

"It is the oldest castle in France, built in the twelfth century."

Isabelle led Alec into a second central point, deep within the Village, where a half-dozen old women had gathered to exchange gossip and watch small children play hopscotch.

"This is like a movie set," said Alec.

They walked back to the main terrace and descended down a stairway to a house. Isabelle opened the door and Alec followed her into the foyer.

"This is La Dame Jeanne," said Isabelle. "They do simple, Provençal cooking."

A casually-dressed maître d' led Alec and Isabelle through two small rooms to a third room and sat them with menus.

"This is a family-run restaurant," said Isabelle. "They live here, upstairs, and everybody works. It is the French way."

A waitress appeared with complimentary glasses of Kir Royal, a specialty of champagne mixed with Cassis, blackcurrant liqueur.

"Now tell me about the book you are writing," said Isabelle.

"I'm at a very early stage. Preliminary research. But if it works, it will be a novel set in Monaco."

"And tell me about your friend."

"Who?" said Alec.

"The man in Le Texan last night. You said you met him at the hotel. But *he* said you had flown here together."

Alec was silent. He was rarely caught out; he must be slipping. That damn dentist!

"I'm working on a very delicate business proposal," said Alec finally. "And the man you met is also involved. I met him just before the flight."

"What kind of business?"

Alec was uncomfortable, but he quickly grew into a legend, a cover story. "I'm consulting for a group that wants to start a lottery in Monaco."

"Oh, you mean tickets that you scratch for a winning number?"

"Like that, but bigger," said Alec. "We want to propose what's known as an 'on-line' lottery, a computerized system with big prizes. We've got to keep it quiet because there's a lot of competition in the lottery business. We want to get a head start in Monaco."

"Is that why you need those books I bought?"

"Partly, yes. And partly for my novel."

"And how is it," said Isabelle, "that a novelist finds himself involved in the lottery business?"

This was going nowhere fast. Alec was glad to be interrupted by a waitress so he could collect his thoughts.

"I've always wanted to write," said Alec, after ordering appetizers. "I'd like to get out of the lottery business to become a full-time writer. And I just may be able to do that if we pull off this deal in Monaco."

Isabelle seemed satisfied.

"Now tell me about yourself," said Alec. "Are you always so curious?"

"Always," said Isabelle.

"And what plans do you have for the future."

"None. I like it here. I enjoy the institut—I like the students."

"What do you do in your spare time?"

"The institut keeps me busy—it has grown so much in a few years. But I play tennis and swim, and I go to the cinema in Nice."

"It sounds like a pleasant life here," said Alec. "I envy you."

"Envy *me*? You're lucky. I'd love to live in America."

"Why?"

"I like Americans. They're so friendly. My boyfriend is American."

Alec's heart dropped like a stone.

"He just left," continued Isabelle. "Went back to America, Arizona. He was only 19, one of my students— too young for me. I need an older man."

The appetizers arrived and Alec ordered a bottle of Pouilly Fumé to compliment their entree, the Loup, sea bass, grilled Provençal style with herbs and olive oil.

Afterwards, they walked up to the terrace overlooking Monaco, and Isabelle led Alec into Les Deux Frères for a nightcap of Armagnac, taken beside the glowing embers in the fireplace. Alec felt only warmth, from the brandy within and the fire nearby. He hadn't enjoyed an evening so much since long before his wife had passed away.

Afterwards, as they stood side by side on the terrace, enjoying the view of Monaco, Alec felt giddy from the wine, wanted to reach over and kiss Isabelle, but he resisted the urge. It was too splendid an evening to spoil with a drunken advance.

"Let's go," said Isabelle. She surprised Alec by grabbing his hand and leading him back down the hill to her car. Isabelle drove to the Moyen Corniche and back to Monaco through Rocquebrune-sur-Mer at the base of Cap Martin, past the Monaco Tennis Club and the Beach Club, along Avenue Princesse Grace to Loews.

"Would you like to come in?" asked Alec.

"Yes," said Isabelle. "You still haven't told me what you need translated."

Isabelle gave her keys to the valet and Alec scooped up his books from the back seat.

They walked into the lobby.

"We can sit in the piano bar or go to my room," said Alec. "I have a private terrace overlooking the sea." Alec felt awkward. He hadn't dated in the two years since his wife died. It had been two decades since he had asked a woman to his room.

"Let's go to your room."

Alec carefully, quietly turned the key in his lock, not wishing to bump into Spinola and not knowing, not caring what, if anything, had transpired between Vinnie and Spinola.

Alec walked straight to the sliding glass door and opened it wide, exposing the cozy terrace. He beckoned Isabelle to join him. "May I offer you a drink?"

"Champagne." Isabelle slipped off her shoes.

Alec found a half-bottle of Moet & Chandon inside the mini-bar. He uncorked the bottle, joined Isabelle on the terrace and poured two glasses of bubbly.

"Here is to your novel." Isabelle raised her glass.

"And to meeting you," said Alec.

"What would you like me to do next?" asked Isabelle.

"Pardon me?"

"The translating. Do you know which pages or chapters you want translated?"

"Oh. Let's look through the books together."

Alec picked up the first volume and Isabelle moved around the table, closer, to Alec's side, and they both leaned over the book.

"Here, the very early history," said Isabelle, "from pages one to twelve." Isabelle faced Alec, her lips only inches from his own, her big brown eyes gazing into his eyes.

Alec could not help himself. He leaned forward to fill the gap and make contact with Isabelle's lips. She closed her eyes and put her arms around his shoulders, and the pair sat kissing for a half-minute. Alec rose, walked a few steps to the railing, looked out to the sea. Isabelle joined him, at his side.

"Is something wrong?" asked Isabelle.

"No, no. Everything is right." Alec turned and kissed her again, and the pair embraced.

"Come," said Isabelle. "Let's go inside." She reached for Alec's hand, as she had in Rocquebrune Village, led him back into the room and sat them both at the foot of the bed.

Alec embraced Isabelle, kissed her lips and explored her mouth with his tongue as Isabelle stroked the back of his head softly. Then Alec kissed her long, silky-smooth neck. Isabelle moaned softly.

Isabelle stood, unbuttoned her blouse and Alec helped it fall gently from her arms. Isabelle unsnapped her bra, let it drop to the floor, and Alec kissed her full, round breasts, allowing his tongue to flicker around her hardened nipples. He moved his lips slowly down Isabelle's torso, to her belly-button, holding her buttocks in his hands. Isabelle reached down behind her, unfastened her short black skirt, and let it fall to her feet. Alec stood back while Isabelle unhitched her black stockings and unrolled them down her legs, exposing a mound of pubic hair, and she stood before him, completely naked, as natural as the day she was born, without a trace of modesty.

"Come," said Isabelle. "Let's get into bed."

Alec slowly unbuttoned his shirt, watching as Isabelle pulled down the cover. He was hard by now, and he felt a tinge of embarrassment as he removed his trousers and boxer shorts, exposing his erection. Why was it, he wondered, Americans were so modest about nudity, about sex, while the French were so relaxed, unburdened by raw human anatomy and its expressions of love?

Alec climbed onto the bed, beside Isabelle, and the pair embraced, kissing, feeling, and slowly, gently, becoming one. Isabelle mounted Alec, and he felt her moistness engulf him, swallow his erection, and she cried out as he thrust himself into her, penetrating her very soul.

Later, as they lay cuddling, arms and legs entangled beneath a sheet, Isabelle brushed her lips against Alec's nipples.

"Are you married?" asked Isabelle.

"Would it matter?"

"No. I'm just curious."

"I used to be married," said Alec. "Nineteen years. My wife died two weeks before our 20th anniversary."

"I'm sorry," said Isabelle.

"So am I," said Alec. "I still miss her."

"Kids?"

"Yes. A boy and a girl, both in college."

Isabelle put her head on Alec's chest and the two fell asleep.

*****

Alec was awakened, as usual, by the morning light streaming through his window. Isabelle was asleep beside him, and he left the bed quietly so as not to awaken her. He wished he could spend the day with her instead of having to deal with Spinola, with Barry Zubrick and maybe even Vinnie if the uncouth cousin hadn't found his flight.

Isabelle stirred, sat up and rubbed her eyes.

"Good morning." Alec appeared at the bathroom door, a large towel wrapped around his body. "Would you like cappucino and croissants?"

Isabelle smiled, nodded, and dived back into her pillows. Alec picked up the phone and dialed room service. A minute after he put down the phone, it rang.

"It's me," snapped Barry Zubrick. "What's the plan?"

"Good morning, Ted," said Alec. "I suppose we'll meet later this morning."

"You *suppose?*"

"Yes, I *suppose* I'll be able to find The Dentist. But God knows where he might be or what shape he might be in. Where shall we meet?"

"We *can't* meet at the usual place any more, can we?"

"If you say not, Ted." Alec was not willing to engage Barry's abrasiveness with anything more than feigned obsequiousness.

"Let's meet at the hotel that starts with H, got it?"

There was only one. Hotel Hermitage. Barry must truly be going nuts. Anyone in Monaco tapping his phone, *if* anyone was tapping his phone, would know it, too.

"Got it," said Alec. "Any special time?"

"11:30 this morning."

"Who was that?" asked Isabelle.

"Lottery business," said Alec.

Isabelle showered and joined Alec on the balcony as room service arrived with a large tray of cappucino and three kinds of sweet rolls. As they sat down they could hear a terrible argument underway in the next room.

"You no-good two-timing shit!" This was a female voice, followed by the smash of something breakable against a wall. "You rob gold out the teeth of poor people!"

A feeble voice tried to deal with the outrage he was facing.

"You scum-sucker! You fuck!" yelled the female. "Who do you think you are, James Bond? You can kiss my ass!"

Spinola had left his sliding door open and the venomous words flew out crystal clear.

"How could you do this to him?" screamed the female. "And you call yourself his cousin? You're a fucking shit!" Another object hit the wall and shattered, and Spinola finally had the presence of mind to close the sliding door.

Two minutes later, a knock at Alec's door. Alec looked at Isabelle, shrugged, and walked to the door, opening it six inches. Spinola stood before him, in a bathrobe.

"What did you do with Vinnie?" the dentist demanded.

"I sent him home," said Alec.

"Whatta mean sent him home? Why'd ya do that? He's my cousin!"

"Don't you remember what happened yesterday afternoon?"

"Oh, shit, that was nuthin'. Me and Vinnie *always* fight like that."

Alec swung his head in disbelief, then faced Spinola. "Look, I don't care how you guys do things in Hoboken . . ."

"But if Vinnie's gone, how am I supposed to sign that agreement?"

Alec looked back at Isabelle, watching from the balcony, opened the door and joined Spinola out in the hall, holding the door only slightly ajar behind him.

"Okay." Alec's face tightened. "Let's get this straight." Vinnie's out of here, and you've got two minutes to decide if you're signing that agreement. I don't care one way or the other, but if you don't decide yes, you're out of here this morning, just like Vinnie, no more money, nothing. And what's all that yelling in your room?"

Spinola looked sheepish. "You heard it?"

"Me and everyone else in Monte Carlo. Who's in there?"

"It's Vic. She's mad about Vinnie. And she thinks I've got a girlfriend here."

"Get rid of her, too. If you don't, I will. Now, what's the decision?"

Spinola shuffled his feet, looked down at the carpet. "Yeah, yeah, I guess I'll sign."

"No guesses," said Alec. "Yes or no."

"Okay, okay—yeah."

"We're meeting with Ted at 11:30," said Alec. "Meet me in the lobby at eleven. And lose that loud-mouthed blond. Permanently."

Alec turned, walked back into the room and rejoined Isabelle on the balcony. "This lottery business is a pain in the behind. If I hadn't met you, I think I'd just turn around and go home." Alec bent down and gave her a kiss on the forehead.

Isabelle collected the books on Monaco, for translation, and left for work, and Alec took a stroll the length of Avenue Princesse Grace, along the marble promenade bordering the cove-shaped public beach. Alec marveled at how glistening clean and fresh everything seemed, and watched as a sanitation crew finished hosing down the street, a morning ritual throughout the principality. He walked as far as the Beach Plaza Hotel, discovered a public *ascenseur* and ascended to the Boulevard des Moulins, Monte Carlo's main shopping street. He perused the shop windows; liked what he saw in Façonnable, a men's clothing boutique specializing in a sporty, collegiate look—the French equivalent of Polo Ralph Lauren. Alec was going to need new clothing; his five-day supply of shirts, socks and underwear would soon run out, and, with a half-million in the bank, it was time to treat himself. And though he didn't admit it to himself, he wanted to look younger, more stylish for Isabelle.

Within forty-five minutes, Alec racked up a double-breasted sport coat, two pairs of pleated khaki trousers, five shirts, six pairs of boxer shorts, six pairs of socks and a belt. He felt good about himself. In control.

Spinola was waiting in the lobby at eleven. "I need cash," he said to Alec.

"We'll sort out some money *after* you sign," said Alec. He was enjoying the new authority that had crept into his soul. "What about the blond?"

"She ain't talkin'-a me," said Spinola. He pointed up. "Bitch. She's at the pool."

"Okay, let's go."

Alec and Spinola were sitting in the Hermitage lobby when Barry arrived at 11:30. He sat down, looked furtively around the lobby, and produced a folded document from inside his jacket pocket.

"I assume," said Barry, "that you are ready to sign?"

"Yeah, yeah," said Spinola. "Sorry about Vinnie—he's a hothead."

Barry rolled his eyes; was tempted to deliver a lecture on personal responsibility, but was more intent on getting his contract signed.

Spinola looked through the agreement again. Barry handed him a pen, and watched impatiently as Spinola read the agreement a second time, slowly studying each word.

"I'm gonna need some cash right away," said Spinola, looking up.

"I have a check for $25,000 drawn on Citibank here in Monaco," said Barry. "All you have to do is open an account there with this check and the funds will be available within a few hours."

Spinola pressed the pen to the document and, with a flourish, signed his name.

"I hope you guys realize," said Spinola, folding the check, "that my family name wasn't always Spinola."

"WHAT?" yelled Barry.

Spinola put the check in his shirt pocket. "It was originally Spinolini. It got changed at Ellis Island when my granddad came to America. Is that a problem?"

Alec sat back, amazed, containing himself from bursting into laughter.

"Oskilamola!" ranted Barry. He created his own lan-

guage when seriously agitated. Barry paused, thinking,
"Well, it's too late to do anything now. As far as I'm
concerned you're a Spinola. Keep the Spinolini business
to yourself."

"Ted," said Alec. "Our whole case for legitimacy is
based on Gerry being a descendant of the Spinola who
once ruled Monaco . . ."

"Spinola, Spinolini, spaghetti . . . it's all the same to
me," snapped Barry. "Who will know? His passport says
Spinola, that's all I care about. And it's not as if he's
really going to take over."

Alec was incredulous; said nothing.

"Do you need me anymore?" asked Spinola. "I think
I'll mosey on over to the bank."

"Not so fast," said Alec. "Why didn't you tell us
sooner about your grandfather?"

"No one asked."

"Why did you answer the *Wall Street Journal* ad?"

"My nephew Stevie saw it. He's a stockbroker. He
thought maybe I had a rich old aunt somewhere who
needed an heir."

"All right," said Alec. "Go to the bank. But after
that, get rid of the blond. Today."

"She don't have her ticket," said Spinola.

"Why not?"

"Vinnie took it with him. She's stuck here."

"You've got plenty of money now. Buy her a ticket."

"Why should *I* spring for it? You're the one who
wants her outta here."

Alec looked at Spinola hard. "I don't care how you
do it. Just get that bimbo on a plane by tonight."

Barry folded the signed agreement and put it into his
jacket pocket.

Spinola rose, grunted and sauntered out the revolving door.

"Alec, I need you to go to London," said Barry. "J.J. is already there, organizing logistics, and I want you to help."

"What about the research I'm doing?"

"I just want you to go for a few days, hook up with J.J., see what's going on, come back and report to me. Then you can finish the research."

Fair enough. It would take Isabelle a few days or more to do the translating he needed. And at least he'd have a break from Spinola.

"When do you want me to leave."

"This afternoon. British Airways has a three o'clock flight. J.J. is at the Stafford Hotel, near St. James's Place. He'll be expecting you."

"Look," said Alec. "I'm not happy about using a Spinola who's really a Spinolini."

"Spinola, Spinolini—what's the big deal. It took us two weeks to find *this* guy. Where the hell we going to dig up another Spinola by the end of the week?"

"But it ruins our case."

"If it makes the damn frogs feel any better we'll find another Spinola later," said Barry. "We're out of time."

Alec tried calling Isabelle, and got as far as leaving a message that he'd be away for a few days; that he'd call upon his return. Alec never liked to tell anyone where he was going. He picked up his ticket from the travel agency inside Loews, packed his garment bag—overstuffed with new purchases—and checked out of the hotel. A Heli Air Monaco shuttle van whisked him to the heliport in Fontvieille. The seven-minute helicopter ride was cheaper for one person travelling alone than a taxi to Nice-Côte d'Azur Airport. And what a glamorous way to travel. Alec studied the scenic coastline; the towns of Beaulieu and St. Jean, and the snow-capped Alps behind them.

And then Alec boarded BA's "Riviera Route" to London.

7

The British Airways Airbus 320 made its final approach through three layers of thick dark cloud, heavy and inert. Alec turned his watch back one hour. It was just past four o'clock, but already dark in London. Dark, gloomy and wet.

"Stafford Hotel, St. James's," Alec told the cab-driver.

Rush hour traffic was at its peak outward bound, but the traffic *into* the West End was merciless anyway. Alec looked out the window at the sad, rainy streets. He did not care for this climate; it depressed him. With any luck he wouldn't have to leave the hotel.

The Stafford was a low-profile hotel deluxe, on a dead-end back street, favored by diplomats and high ranking military officials. Even London's cabbies, who were supposed to know every street in the city, were hard-pressed to find the Stafford, owned by the Ritz a few blocks away.

Alec checked in, was shown to his room. J.J. was out and had not left a message, so Alec dined alone in the hotel restaurant, then retired to his room to watch the nine o'clock news on BBC One.

Alec was dozing, the TV still on, when he heard a

rap on his door. He jumped up, put his hand on the doorknob. "Who is it?"

"J.J."

Alec opened the door and General John J. Stemmer stood before him, a thick, unlit cigar sticking almost horizontally out the left side of his mouth. J.J. had a stubble of a crew cut, half gray, half bald. He was still in command of middle age. "Glad you made it, kid."

* * * * *

General Stemmer was the first person Barry Zubrick had called after his visit to Monaco's wax museum. The general had been retired just over a year, forced out by the president for his controversial views opposing troop cutbacks in Europe. He was all for keeping thousands of American troops in Germany; not to defend Europe from the former Soviet Union—he fully appreciated that the Cold War was over—but to protect Germany from itself. But nobody wanted to hear about German atrocities anymore. And so J.J. was given final marching orders; exiled overnight to his quiet stone farmhouse outside of Charlottesville, Virginia.

Barry had called his old high school buddy, asked him to fly to Monaco for a meeting and, with little else to do except sit on his porch, the general obliged his eccentric friend.

Barry was not one to waste words—he laid out the problem within five minutes of sitting down with the general inside the lobby of Hotel Metropole.

Like most of Barry's deals, it was simple, straightforward and based on a handshake—and that's the only time Barry liked to shake hands; a million bucks for J.J. for staging a coup; a second million for success.

The general reserved his answer until he'd spent two days walking the principality's streets, looking at maps, pinpointing targets, devising tactics and strategy. He walked during the day, he walked at night, getting a feel for the *rhythm* of the place. And then he had given his assent.

"I can do it," J.J. said. "I think it can be done in 30 minutes. Taking Monaco will be easy. The challenge will be keeping it. We need a plan for dealing with France."

J.J. and Barry had brainstormed a variety of possibilities.

"Can't we place biological bombs, like anthrax, in a few French cities?" said Barry. "Threaten to set them loose if they won't play ball?"

"Extremely difficult logistically," said the general. "Terrorists would have tried it years ago if it was remotely possible. *And* you'd probably have to detonate one to get them to take you seriously. Thousands would die horrible deaths and *you* would be painted as the worst nightmare since Saddam Hussein."

"How about sabotaging a French nuclear reactor?" Barry asked.

"I don't think anything like that will be necessary," said J.J. after considering the matter. "Subtlety and illusion will be our best weapons. We'll want a contingency, but I'm beginning to think we can do business with the French. They always have their own best interest at heart, and we can certainly shape this to make it worth their while to work with us."

Barry was intrigued. Diplomacy had never been his strong suit and that, perhaps, was why the world had grown so small for him. When it came to adversaries, he knew nothing but confrontation. His motto could have been "Fight and run."

"I caught wind of something to do with the French back in Washington, on the spook cocktail circuit," said J.J. "I'd like to go back to Washington and check out a few things."

J.J. had flown home, made a few calls, connected with several old friends in the intelligence community. He pinned down the rumors he had heard, verified them twice with co-members of the Pinay Circle, his elite little "think-tank" of former generals and high-level spooks. And then he returned to Europe to plan the operation.

*****

Alec knotted a tie around his neck, pulled on a blazer and followed J.J. down to the Stafford bar.

"The best thing about this hotel is their selection of scotch whiskey," said J.J. "Care to join me?"

Alec nodded and J.J. ordered the Macallan for them both. "No ice, a few drops of mineral water," J.J. instructed the bartender.

"You're going to meet Piers Furnivall," said J.J. "He was in the SAS—you know, the British Special Air service. Colonel Furnivall is supplying the manpower for our op. And tomorrow we're going to arrange for the weapons. Here's the shopping list." J.J. handed Alec a worn piece of lined paper full of his scribblings. As Alec perused the notes, Furnivall entered the bar.

"Piers Furnivall, Alec Perry." The men shook hands and J.J. ordered Sterling a Macallan.

"We're set," whispered the colonel. "Thirty-five men, 26 are ex-SAS, three from SBS for the marine work, a handful of South Africans and a couple of chopper pilots." SBS was the Special Boat Service, the British equivalent to US Navy SEALS.

"Good, good," said J.J., chomping on his cigar furiously. "And transportation logistics?"

"I've staggered them on eight different flights over three days," said Furnivall. "They're checking into several hotels in the Nice area, then arriving at different hours throughout the day at the Vista Palace on Friday for our `convention.' None of them know the final destination, the op. We have Friday night and Saturday to go over the nuts and bolts."

J.J. nodded in appreciation, exhaled air as if it were cigar smoke.

"Are we straight on weapons?" asked the colonel.

"Under control," said J.J.

"How long will our men need to be there?" asked Furnivall.

"One week minimum, maybe two." J.J. raised his glass, drained the Macallan.

"Any escape contingency?"

"If there's any problem taking Monaco—and there won't be—we literally head for the hills. The Italian border, only a few miles away."

Colonel Furnivall's company, the Sterling Group, which normally specialized in counter-terrorism training, had been on the verge of bankruptcy until J.J. came along.

*****

Next morning, Alec found himself on an Inter-City express train with J.J. heading north, digging into a traditional English breakfast of eggs, kippers, sausage, tomato, mushrooms, toast and marmalade, and endless cups of Earl Grey tea.

They were on their way to Birmingham to meet with J.J.'s old friend, Livingston Momus, who owned a huge warehouse of weapons—the largest private arsenal in Europe. The problem J.J. faced was not the purchase of weapons—he had already obtained a permit on behalf of the Sri Lankan government, which routinely bought weapons through middlemen like J.J. to deal with Tamil separatists—but getting them to the Vista Palace Hotel near Monaco.

It would be too risky to ferry a van of weapons over the Channel and take pot luck with French Customs. And too logistically complex to fly them to France—or anywhere in Europe. J.J. decided the best route was by boat. Charter a private yacht in Southampton and sail it to Menton, ten miles from Monaco, near the Italian border, where Customs was relatively lax.

A representative of Globalarms met J.J. and Alec at the train station and drove them to the warehouse and its suite of offices. Liv Momus, a grizzly bear of a man, was dressed like a banker, in a conservative navy blue suit and heavy black shoes.

"If it ain't J.J. Stemmer, in the flesh!" said Momus, a fellow American. He walked over and gave the general a bear hug. "It's always a pleasure. And you're still blowin' on that old cee-gar—Har, Har, Har!" And when he laughed, his whole body shook. "And who be you?"

Alec offered his hand to Momus. "Alec Perry—a pleasure to meet you."

"Well, boys," drawled Momus, returning to his desk. "Sit on down. What can ah do for you today?"

J.J. handed over his scribblings and Momus scanned the shopping list.

"Kalishnikovs, Heckler and Koch, M26 grenades ... RPG-7 portable rocket launchers? Jeez, they's gettin' serious over there. You got paperwork?"

J.J. snapped open his attache case and pulled out a

sheaf of papers in a manilla file, handed it across the desk to Momus, who perused the documents carefully. "Yep," said Momus. "Everything looks in order here. When you boys want delivery?"

"Tomorrow," said J.J. "In Southampton."

"Ain't the best weather for a fishin' trip," said Momus.

"Can't be helped," said J.J. "That's how they want it this time."

J.J. pulled a $25,000 check from his pocket and handed it to Momus. It was drawn on a Zurich bank, and the fact that it was signed by Barry Zubrick did not phase Livingston Momus for a second. He was accustomed to all kinds of circuitous payments for arms. If the paperwork was in order, it mattered not from where or whom the money was coming.

"Y'all come back soon," said Momus, rising. "Give my assistant the destination details. Your equipment will arrive tomorrow afternoon between four and five."

J.J. and Alec caught a train back to London. Alec watched the gloomy landscape—dark cloud, rain— through the train's window and thought of Monaco's blue sky and brilliant sunshine. He thought of Isabelle.

"Do you need me in Southampton?" asked Alec.

"Not really," said J.J. "I didn't even need you for this, 'cept I'm glad you met Piers Furnivall. You know Barry. He doesn't trust no one. I suppose he thinks we'll watch each other." He chuckled to himself. "He's a crazy old bird. God knows what he'll do with Monaco."

"How did he get the way he is?" asked Alec.

"Oh, Barry's always been different," said J.J. "And *different* is putting it lightly. Even back in high school, an agenda all his own, driving everyone crazy. That was Barry." J.J. shook his head.

"Was he popular?"

"You kidding? He was an outcast. I think he was born an outcast—he wouldn't have it any other way— and he ran a gang of rejects who couldn't get into anyone else's gang. Everyone called them *The Zubes*. But he was no dunce. And he hated authority—teachers, the principal— he plotted against them constantly, directing The Zubes to pull off quirky acts of sabotage. You know, he once published his own underground newspaper—a one-off—and Barry, the sly bastard that he is, managed to get it printed on the school's own mimeograph machine! Can you beat that? Got some woman in the print room to believe it was a school-sponsored student paper. Yeah, even back then he used that funny written language of his."

"You mean the phonetical stuff?" asked Alec. "Why?"

"Typical Barry," said J.J. "He says that English has evolved badly, and he's made it one of his missions in life to single-handedly revamp written English, all based on phonetics. He drove our English teacher nuts. He drove *all* the teachers nuts."

"Where does the paranoia come from?" asked Alec.

"It's innate. That's all I can figure. Look, you got a guy who one day complains to the English teacher about why it makes more sense spelling the word could c-u-d instead of c-o-u-l-d, and then he publishes a so-called 'anonymous' underground newspaper using all his pho-netical spellings, and then he wonders how they know it's him! He blamed The Zubes—Har, Har! He thought one of them turned him in!"

Alec winced. "And that's a guy who's supposed to run Monaco?"

"Hell, he's paying me good to do what I'm best at. What do I care if the spoiled old Grimaldis get tossed out of Monaco? They don't mean a hill of beans to me. I can get my tired ass back to Charlottesville and retire in comfort."

"You have no doubts about success?" asked Alec.

"Like I said before," said J.J. "Taking Monaco is a cinch. The last thing they ever expect is a coup. With an element of surprise, we'll be calling the shots in less than an hour. The problem all along has been France. But I don't think they're going to be much of a problem after all." J.J. smiled.

"Why not?"

"We're gonna deal with them, and make them a deal they'll like—but we needed a fallback, something to nail it down in case they get stubborn, something those Frenchies are good at. I found out something that'll knock their socks off—our ace in the hole."

"And that is?"

Alec listened intently as J.J. whispered what he had on France.

*****

Back at Loews late that evening, the first call Alec made was to Isabelle.

"Alec? Where are you?"

"I'm in Monaco. I had to go to London on business. I hope it's not too late to call?"

"No. I've been working on your translation. It will be finished by tomorrow if I keep working."

"Okay. I was hoping we could meet, but it's better if you keep at it," said Alec. "Dinner tomorrow night?"

"Yes, everything should be done. I'll come to Loews about 7:30."

Alec buzzed Spinola's room. No answer. He grabbed

his new sport coat and went down to the lobby, into the casino, searching for the dentist. He checked out the piano bar, Café de la Mer and the Restaurant Pistou on the top floor and its mini-casino. Still no Spinola.

Alec walked out to the Café de Paris. It was now past 11 p.m. and Place du Casino bustled with late night sightseers. Some kind of gala was taking place at the Hotel de Paris and its forecourt was chock-a-block with Bentleys, Ferraris and stretch Mercedes limousines; people-watchers were out in force, mostly on the Café de Paris terrace, which afforded a fine view of the action.

Alec sat down and ordered an Armagnac. Its flavor reminded him of Isabelle, of Rocquebrune Village. He felt good to be back in Monaco. The very thought of London made him shiver.

As Alec watched a throng of picture-taking tourists on the steps of the Grand Casino, it hit him that Spinola was probably inside, gambling away his new fortune. He drained his glass, walked over and paid the 50-franc admission to get in. It was quite different from the casino at Loews—antiquated, elegant garland and gilt. At least you could enjoy the scenery while you lost your money.

Alec walked into the main gambling hall and imme-diately glimpsed the dentist—he was tough to miss in a mauve suit—at a high-stakes roulette table. As he walked toward the table, Alec noticed Vicky standing near the dentist. The warmth inside Alec's gut turned to indiges-tion—he thought he'd been very clear about losing the blond. As he approached Spinola, he could see the dentist was sweating bullets, wiping his forehead with a handker-chief, face twitching, oblivious to Alec's presence until Alec stood right next to him and tapped his shoulder.

Spinola jumped. "Alec! Where've ya been?"

"Out of town. Can we have a word?" Alec motioned to a corner nearby.

"Yeah, yeah—after the next spin."

Alec watched Spinola stack different colored chips on assorted numbers, a column, red—changing his selections in a frenzy as the wheel turned. The tiny silver ball fell into a slot and the croupier scooped up most of the chips, replenishing few.

"Damn!" Spinola cursed. "I shoulda stuck to craps. Damn frogs don't play that in here."

The croupier and a few other players threw unpleasant glances at the dentist.

"Where ya goin', honey?" hollered Vicky as Spinola followed Alec to a corner. "Oh, hiya Alec!"

"I'll be back," said Spinola. "Just stay put."

Alec faced the dentist. "I thought I told you to get rid of the blond?"

"Whatta you, my mother? She says she wants to stay a week. What am I supposed to do? You think I want her around with all these gorgeous broads?" Spinola waved his arms at the beautiful women who crowded the tables.

"She can't stay a week," said Alec. "She has to be out of here tomorrow."

"*You* tell her. She won't listen to *me*."

"Have you at least bought her a ticket?"

Spinola leaned over, grabbed Alec's elbow and spoke lower. "I don't have the dough."

"What do you mean?"

"Ya know, moulah—it's gone."

"All thirty grand?" Alec looked wide-eyed at the dentist, incredulous.

Spinola shrugged. "Yeah, I think everything's rigged. And something else."

"What?"

"That guy's been following me." Spinola pointed to a young man in a sport coat and slacks who stood about 50 yards away, near a roulette table, and who turned quickly when the dentist pointed and Alec looked over.

"Jesus Christ!" said Alec. "How long has this been going on?"

"I dunno. I just noticed him tonight. I saw him at Loews, then I saw him here, lookin' at me."

"This is what I want you to do," said Alec. "And by God, just do it, no questions. Get Vicky—wait a second, have you told Vicky *anything* about why you're here?"

"No, no. No way. Well, just a little."

Alec shook his head and grimaced. "You stupid shit. Okay. Get Vicky and go back to Loews, to your room. Stay put until you hear from me. Got it?"

"Ah, hell, I shouldn't-a said nuthin'," said Spinola. "I gotta win my money back."

"No," said Alec firmly. "Leave now. I'll catch up with you later. Do it—now!"

Alec stood back and watched as Spinola trudged back to his table.

"C'mon Vic, we gotta go."

"Go where? I'm just startin' to have fun."

"I'm serious, Vic. I'm goin' back to my room."

"What? It's not even midnight. You're gettin' to be such an old fart, Spinny. Can't we have a nightcap?"

"No. I mean, look, I'll order up a bottle of champagne in the room."

"Oh, Spinny, you're soooo romantic. Why didn't you say so?"

Alec watched as Spinola and Vicky left; watched as the young man in the sport coat followed them out at a discreet distance. Alec followed the surveillant to Loews; saw the dentist and Vicky ascend in an elevator while the young man appeared to study a display window of fine watches. Then the man pulled a small radio-phone from inside his jacket and spoke into it.

Alec walked back outside, wondering if he, too, was under surveillance, and decided to take a long walk, see if anyone followed. He walked down to Avenue Princesse Grace, along the beachfront promenade, stopping periodically to detect surveillance. Nothing. He walked on, past the Beach Plaza Hotel to the Sporting d'Ete, an entertainment complex that housed Jimmy'z, Monaco's top discotheque. He turned the corner into the jet-setting playground and stood near a palm tree. No one followed. Alec turned back, found the public ascenseur and ascended to Boulevard des Moulins, past Façonnable, the men's boutique, and back to Loews. The young man was no longer in the lobby.

Alec went up to the fourth floor and knocked on Spinola's door. No answer. He knocked again, louder.

"Who's there?" He heard Spinola's voice, a giggle in the background.

"Alec."

Spinola opened the door, disheveled in a bathrobe. "Kerist, Alec—we're gettin' it on in here. Whatta ya want now?"

"Sorry, never mind," said Alec. "I'll catch you in the morning."

Alec returned to his room, laid down on his bed fully clothed, adrenalin pumping, head throbbing. He was trying to think it all through: What was going on? Had Spinola been talking about the plan? Or Vinnie, seeking revenge? Maybe the surveillance was simply related to the dentist's gambling habits. Alec slept badly while his

subconscious tried to thrash out the new stimuli with a
round of bad dreams. He awoke in a cold sweat just
before 6 a.m., rose and showered, and took cappucino
out on the balcony. The caffeine put him into gear. First
step, he had to get Spinola out of Monaco; contain whatever damage had been done; move him to Nice, a big city
full of anonymous hotels. That would solve the Vicky
problem, too. If they followed him all the way to Nice,
Alec reasoned, they were all in serious trouble. If there
was no surveillance outside the principality, then it was
probably routine surveillance of an erratic gambler of
dubious credit. One thing was certain: Alec didn't want
to be seen with Spinola again.

Alec waited till eight, then knocked on the dentist's
door. He knocked a second time, and a groggy Spinola
opened the door.

"You again?" said Spinola.

"Get up, get dressed, get packed," said Alec. "You're
moving."

"Whattaya talkin' about?" Spinola was annoyed.

With a rapid movement, Alec pushed his arm straight
out, his open palm landing square on Spinola's chest, and
the dentist fell back into the room, followed by Alec, who
closed the door behind him. Vicky, beneath a mound of
covers and pillows, stirred and lifted her head.

"What's goin' on?" Vicky sat up, covered her boobs.

Alec ignored her. He reached down, grabbed Spinola
by the scruff of his neck and pushed him into a chair.

"I've had enough of your garbage," said Alec. "Listen up, and don't talk back. Pack your things. You're
checking out and moving to Nice."

"What's goin' on, Spinny?" shouted Vicky. "Why are
you lettin' him boss you around like that?"

"Shut-up!" Spinola yelled at Vicky.

"Don't tell me to shut-up, you little shit!" yelled Vicky.

Alec turned and faced Vicky. "*I'm* telling you to shut-up. And if you don't, you're going over the balcony."

Vicky dived under the covers. Alec turned back to Spinola.

"I want you to take a taxi to the Abela Hotel on the Boulevard des Anglais," said Alec. "Got it? Write it down." Alec grabbed a pencil and pad from the desk and handed it to the dentist. "Abela. They'll be expecting you. Any questions?"

"Yeah," said Spinola. "How am I supposed to pay for it?"

"Are you completely broke?"

"Yeah, yeah."

"All thirty grand?"

"Yeah, yeah. Don't rub it in."

Alec shook his head in disbelief. He reached into his pocket and pulled out a wad of currency, from which he pulled four 500-franc notes. "Here. This'll take care of the taxi and a few meals. The room will be on a credit card. Stay near the hotel—I'll be out later to see you."

Alec went downstairs, picked up a *Herald Tribune* at the newspaper shop and parked himself down the lobby, near the piano bar, far enough away from the check-out desk so Spinola wouldn't see him.

Spinola and the blond appeared 45 minutes later. The lobby was quiet at this hour—about nine o'clock—and Alec did not detect any surveillance of Spinola. He watched as Spinola and Vicky exited the hotel and got into a taxi, then he walked out to the forecourt as the taxi rounded a corner and pulled away. No one else around. Alec exhaled, relieved, walked back to his room.

The phone was ringing, and it stopped before he could reach it. A minute later it began ringing again and Alec scooped up the receiver.

"Alec? It's me, Ted."

"Good morning, Ted. We should meet."

"Eleven-thirty," said Ted. "The H place. Got it?"

"Yes, Ted. Got it."

Alec set off at ten, took a long walk down to the port, strolled a few backstreets, stopping, watching for reflections in plate glass windows, doubling back a few times. And he stopped at a bakery on Rue Grimaldi for a cappucino, watched the passersby from a small table at the rear. If anyone was following him, they were invisible. Confident now, Alec walked back to Monte Carlo, avoiding the public ascenseur and its cameras, choosing to tackle the hill. He and Barry arrived simultaneously, meeting each other on Square Beaumarchais in front of the Hermitage. They exchanged brief greetings, and Alec followed Ted through the revolving door into the Hermitage lobby. They sat down.

"The dentist has been under surveillance," said Alec.

"WHAT?" Barry's eyes opened wide in horror.

"He was being followed last night in the Casino, right back to . . ."

"I knew it! I knew it! I knew it!" said Barry. "Those nosy toads—they listen to everything!"

"Calm down," said Alec. "It may have nothing to do with you, with the op. Christ, after that fight with his cousin in the Metropole and his drinking, I'm not surprised they're . . ."

"Where is he now?" Barry cut in.

"I've sent him to Nice. We had to get him out of Monaco. *And* he's broke."

"He's what?" said Barry.

"Gambled all the money you gave him—it's gone."

"All of it?"

"Every last franc," said Alec. "I had to give him cab fare—the hotel in Nice is on my credit card."

Barry shook his head. "Stupid man. Never mind, he's more cooperative when he's broke. We still need him. Tell me about J.J."

"It went smoothly," said Alec. "Manpower begins arriving today. Supplies by boat on Thursday."

Barry nodded. With four days to go, everything was on schedule. In 96 hours, Barry would finally have his own country. "Do we have our press release yet?" asked Barry.

"Still working on it," said Alec.

*****

As Barry Zubrick walked out of the Palais de la Scala after collecting his mail, a hand tapped him lightly on the shoulder from behind.

"Excuse me," said a voice, obviously American. "Are you Mister Zubrick?"

"Uh yes, I mean no, what do you want?" snapped Barry, backing off. Barry looked like an overgrown Boy Scout in his baggy shorts, knee socks and Panama hat.

"I'm Bill Blade of the *Miami Herald* and I wonder if . . ."

"Good God!" Barry turned on his heel and trotted off. Barry had a saying about reporters: They should first be drawn and quartered—*then* be permitted to ask questions.

Blade walked after him. "I wonder if we could talk for a few minutes?"

"No, no! I've got nothing to say!" shouted Barry.

"It's important that I get your side of the story." Blade trotted alongside Barry.

"Stop following me!" yelled Barry.

"Mister Zubrick, I really need to talk to you."

"Leave me alone! Or I'll call the cops!"

After another 20 steps, Barry looked back. Blade had stopped. He was holding a camera and snapping pictures.

"You wiener!" yelled Barry. "You can't photograph me! It's an invasion of my privacy!"

"Say 'cheese,' Mister Zubrick!" hollered Blade, cocky now.

Barry covered his face with the palm of his hand, hollered through his fingers, "I'll buy your paper and fire your ass!"

"Good line," goaded Blade, scribbling into a notebook. "Now can we talk?"

Barry walked back to Blade, made a move for the camera, but the reporter was too quick for him; popped the film cartridge out the back and shoved it into his pants pocket.

"What the hell is it you want to know?" demanded Barry. "Can't you see I'm busy?"

"Gary Lincoln spilled out his guts," said Blade. "He says you're a crook. My paper has sent me all this way to get your side of the story."

Barry realized that his last fax must have incited Lincoln to make good on his threat to paint Barry as a villain and turn "Liberty is Us" into a full-fledged scandal.

"Gary Lincoln is a weasel!" hollered Barry. "If you print his lies, I'll sue him for slander and you for libel!"

"That's exactly why we want to hear it from you," said Blade. "Can we have a cup of coffee somewhere?"

"I haven't got time for this," said Barry. "The market opens in 20 minutes!"

"Maybe we can meet later. I'm staying at Loews and ..."

"Wait a second," Barry interrupted. "What has Lincoln told you about me?"

"I'd be happy to tell you. Can't we have a cup of coffee somewhere?"

Barry consulted his watch. "All right. But it's got to be quick." Barry led Blade across Place du Casino to the indoor arcade at Café de Paris. They sat at a small round table.

"Are you still an investment consultant?" asked Blade.

"Never mind that," barked Barry. "Tell me about Lincoln."

Blade flipped open his notebook to an earlier section, its pages covered with inky-blue notations.

"'Lincoln said that 'Liberty is Us' was your idea, that you talked him into fronting for it as a cover for arms trading."

"WHAT?"

"He said you wanted to buy and sell arms using other people's money for down-payments, and that he only found out your motives by accident."

"He's a scoundrel!" yelled Barry. "None of it's true. He tried to blackmail me for more money," Barry blurted, "and I wouldn't budge, so now he's trying to blacken my good name!"

Blade scribbled furiously into his notebook.

"Stop writing my words down!" screamed Barry. "This is off-the-record!"

"You never said that," said Blade.

"I'm saying it now," snapped Barry. "This meeting is over." Barry rose.

"One more thing," said Blade. "Lincoln also said you're planning a coup?"

Barry froze, turned white, sank back down in his chair. "He said WHAT?"

Blade noted the reaction. "He said that you're planning to overthrow a government—which government, Mister Zubrick?"

Blade was good. But Barry immediately realized that Lincoln didn't know—couldn't have known—it was purely coincidence.

"You tell me, Bill Blade," said Barry. "You're the one with all the answers."

Blade took a shot, impulsively. "Mozambique?"

Barry laughed, confident now. Blade didn't know anything. "You're being taken for a fool, Bill Blade. I hope your paper prints Lincoln's donkey dust because I'll win a fortune."

"But Mister Zubrick," said Blade. "How can you sue us if you won't come to the United States?"

"This meeting is over." Barry rose again. As he walked out of the arcade, Blade followed at a discreet distance. Barry assumed Blade would follow him to see where he lived. He walked to the top level of the Galerie Metropole and descended the escalator, down two more floors—caught Blade out the corner of his eye, one floor up—then jumped into an elevator and ascended two floors to the lobby of the Metropole Hotel. He jumped into another elevator, ascended one floor, and walked briskly down a hall, through the pool terrace and out the back door. He sprinted across Avenue Grande-Bretagne and zipped into his apartment building.

Bill Blade stood inside the Metropole's large empty lobby, wondering how the hell Barry Zubrick had disappeared so fast.

*****

To thwart any possible surveillance, Alec called Isabelle to ask her to meet him in the piano bar at the Beach Plaza Hotel instead of picking him up at Loews.

She arrived at 7:45 and joined Alec in the near-empty bar. He was sipping a dry martini, listening to Cole Porter tunes. He rose, returned her greeting—a kiss on each cheek—then hugged her close.

Isabelle sat down, smiled, and lit a cigarette—the only thing about her that Alec didn't like. "Do you like *Chinois* food?"

"Chinese?" said Alec. "Love it."

"There's a good restaurant in Menton. Shall we go?"

Alec drained his drink, paid the check, and the pair walked out the Beach Plaza to Isabelle's car.

"I never realized Monaco was so interesting until I read these books," said Isabelle as she drove through Rocquebrune-sur-Mer. "Your lottery business should work well here. How is it coming?"

"Fine," said Alec. "But it's still too early to tell. As soon as our competitors find out what's we're doing, they'll swarm over with better deals—it's a cut-throat business."

"I haven't translated everything," said Isabelle. "That would take weeks. Just the main points, but I think it's what you want."

Alec sat back, relaxed, content—everything was all right when he was sitting in Isabelle's car, she driving, the magnificent scenery unfolding before his eyes.

"This is it." Isabelle parked in front of The Mandarin. They went in, sat down among the bonsai trees and fish tanks, and Alec ordered a bottle of Bandol rosé wine.

Isabelle reached into her large canvas bag and pulled a sheaf of papers. "I organized the translation into three parts like you asked. One, Monaco's financial arrangement with France; two, French officials in the Monaco government, and three, Monaco's history and the Grimaldi family lineage."

"Well done. Don't read the translation, just tell me about each in your own words."

"D'accord," said Isabelle. "It's strange, but though Monaco is known as a tax haven, most of its revenue comes from tax, which it splits with France. There is no income tax or property tax, but there is a value added tax of 33 percent built into almost everything you buy. Monaco splits this income equally with France. Most people think Monaco prospers from gambling, but gambling accounts for only four-point-five percent of its revenue. Most of it comes from tax." Isabelle studied her notes. "I've heard at the institut there is some question about what will happen in the future, if Europe forces Monaco to lower its value added tax in line to match sales tax in other European countries. Some have said that Monaco will make up the difference by creating an income tax for its foreign residents."

"How seriously is that taken?" asked Alec.

"No one is leaving yet," said Isabelle. "But it's assumed it could lead to a mass exodus. What worries foreign residents is that Monaco would make a tax retroactive by a year, then freeze all Monaco bank accounts to stop people from transferring their accounts to Switzerland or elsewhere."

Alec pulled a pad of paper from inside his jacket and jotted a few notes.

"It is thought," said Isabelle, "that the prince feels taken advantage of by the foreign community. He apparently believes that people should live in Monaco because they like it, not just to escape taxes where they're from. And so, if they had to pay 40 percent tax if they stayed in their own country, they shouldn't mind paying only 10 percent tax to live in Monaco.

"Maybe that's why they want a lottery," added Isabelle. "Then they wouldn't need a tax."

Alec nodded. "You catch on pretty quick."

A waiter brought egg rolls, and Alec had never seen them served in such an appetizing fashion—eight rolls, small and crispy, served with lettuce, mint leaves and a piquant sauce.

"Like this," said Isabelle. She wrapped a leaf of lettuce around an egg roll and a mint leaf, and dipped it into the tangy sauce. Alec did the same, and took a bite.

"Superb," said Alec.

Isabelle turned back to her notes. "The most important French official in Monaco is the Minister of State. He is chosen by the prince from three candidates offered by France. It is an important position in government and he also acts as Monaco's liaison with France. The chief of police is French and so is the chief justice of Monaco's supreme court."

Alec scribbled into his notebook.

"There is more detail on these things," said Isabelle. "I'm just telling you the main points."

"Fine.

"Now the history," said Isabelle. "The name Monaco comes from Monoikos, a tribe of Ligurians who lived on the Rock in the fifth century B.C., though some people think it came from Monachus, the Latin word for monk. Because when the first Grimaldi took control of Monaco, in 1297, he dressed as a monk. That's why the Monaco coat of arms shows two monks with swords. Monaco's independence was recognized by the French in 1489 and by the Spanish in 1613. Back then, Menton and Rocquebrune were part of Monaco, and its revenue came from olives and lemons. After the French Revolution, the French took control of Monaco and turned the palace into a hospital for French soldiers. The French gave Monaco back to the Grimaldis in 1815, and Sardinia took over as its protector. About forty years later, the French helped Austria defeat Sardinia in a war and once again became Monaco's protector. But Menton and Rocquebrune voted to join France, so Monaco lost its source of revenue. That's when they decided to build casinos and have gambling, which was illegal in France.

"In 1911, Prince Albert 1st created a constitution and ended absolute power—in theory.

"Relations with France have been good, except in 1962 there was a major disagreement with De Gaulle."

"What happened in 1962?" asked Alec.

"General De Gaulle didn't like French citizens escaping French tax by moving to Monaco. He demanded that Monaco stop giving tax-free status to French people. It isn't in the history book, but the prince supposedly slapped the French Minister of State and De Gaulle responded by putting a manned border around Monaco and threatened to cut off utility services from France. France made its point. Monaco backed down, and they compromised. All French citizens in Monaco before 1962 were allowed to keep their tax-free status. But from then on, French citizens who moved to Monaco would have to pay French tax."

"And the Grimaldis?" asked Alec.

"Ah, yes. Their last name isn't really Grimaldi any more," said Isabelle.

"What do you mean?"

"The Grimaldi male lineage died out in the early 1700s. A Grimaldi princess married James Matignon of Paris. Today's direct male line descends from the Matignons and the Polignacs, not the Grimaldis."

Alec made a few notes, but realized the name discrepancy would have no relevance. Many royal families of Europe had been through similar name changes, including the most royal of all, the British royal family, whose name Windsor was made up out of thin air to disguise the family's German roots during World War I. Their true name was Hanover, and purists might argue that their original family name was Guelph.

"And what arrangement exists between Monaco's royal family and France?" asked Alec.

"France respects Monaco's sovereignty as long as the Grimaldis keep producing heirs," said Isabelle. "But if the line ever dies out, Monaco reverts to French rule."

The main course arrived, a selection of succulent, aromatic dishes, accompanied by boiled rice and sauteed noodles, and the pair scooped an agglomeration of chicken and pecan nuts, snow-peas, *shitake* mushrooms, and a shrimp and noodles—*My Sao*—onto their plates.

"You've done very well," said Alec.

"Thank you," said Isabelle. "I hope it is of use to your lottery. *And* your book."

"You can never have enough information. Every detail counts for something."

After dinner, Alec and Isabelle took a stroll along the promenade bordering Menton's beachfront, to the old town, then drove back to Loews. On their way to the elevator, Alec thought he glimpsed Spinola in the casino.

"Wait just a minute," he said to Isabelle, venturing inside the casino to check it out. There he was, the goddam dentist, standing at a craps table, with that blond Vicky at his side. Alec stormed over, grabbed Spinola's arm and pulled him away a few steps.

"What the hell are you doing here?" hissed Alec.

"Whattaya talkin' about?" whined Spinola. "I did what you said. I've just come back to gamble—this is the only place where my credit is good."

"I said to stay put in Nice, not come back here!"

"All right, all right," said Spinola, "so I did *half* what you said. What's the big deal?"

"The big deal is that you were being followed last night!" Alec suddenly became cognizant of the possibility that he and Spinola were being watched. "You asshole. Wait five minutes after I leave, then split."

"But I'm ahead!" whined Spinola. "I can't leave now!"

Vicky came up from behind the dentist. "Is he tellin' you what to do again, Spinny?"

Alec rolled his eyes, then locked them with Spinola's. "I'm coming back down here in ten minutes. If you're not gone . . ." Alec shook his head, "serious trouble."

Alec returned to Isabelle and they ascended to his room and uncorked a half-bottle of Moet & Chandon from the mini-bar. Then Alec rode the elevator back down, explored the casino. Spinola was gone.

*****

At 4 a.m., Alec's phone rang. Isabelle stirred, Alec picked it up and heard a shrill woman's voice.

"Ya gotta help me! They got Spinny!"

"What?" said Alec, waking. "Who is this?"

"It's Vicky! They got Spinny—you gotta do something!"

"Who has him?"

"The police! They took him away!"

Alec's heart jumped into his mouth. "Where are you?"

"Downstairs. In the lobby."

"Stay there. I'll be down."

Alec jumped out of bed, pulled on his trousers.

Isabelle sat up. "What's the matter, Alec? Where are you going?"

"There's been a problem. I have to go downstairs. I won't be long." He kissed Isabelle on the forehead.

Vicky was the only person in the lobby, aside from a skeleton crew of two behind the reception counter. She looked dishevelled and smelled of gin. Vicky ran to Alec.

"Shhh." Alec held his forefinger to his lips. "Follow me." He led Vicky back to the piano bar, empty and dark. "What exactly is going on?"

"The police took Spinny away!" whined Vicky.

"Where did it happen?"

"A nightclub."

"Which one? Where?"

"Here. Down the road. It's called Morocco or something."

"Did they arrest him?"

"I don't know, they just *took* him."

"Why? What did he do?"

"I DON'T KNOW!" shrieked Vicky. "Aren't you gonna *do* something?"

"Easy," said Alec. "How many police were there?"

"Four. Four or five. It happened so fast."

"Where did you go after I left?" asked Alec.

"We went to the other casino, the fancy one, ya know. Played roulette. Then we went out to dance."

"Anything happen?" asked Alec. "Did he have an argument with anyone?"

"No, nothin' like that. We was havin' fun—Spinny was winning. And then they just came and took him. You shoulda seen the look on his face—he looked scared, poor Spinny. All he said was, 'get Alec'."

Alec grimaced. "Okay, here's what I want you to do. Here's 500 francs. Take a taxi back to the hotel in Nice. I'll call you later this morning when I find out what's going on."

"Can't I stay here and wait?"

"No. It's better if you go, get some sleep," said Alec. "I'll sort it out and call you."

Alec put Vicky into a taxi and returned to his room. Isabelle was sleeping and Alec crawled in beside her, but could only lay awake, half-expecting a knock on the door any second. Spinola was perfectly capable of telling all about Alec, about Barry, about the plan to launch a coup and oust the Grimaldis from Monaco.

Alec considered picking up and leaving—the last thing he wanted was for Isabelle to be caught up in trouble brought on by this intrigue. But he checked the time—now 5 a.m.—and reasoned that she'd be gone soon—she would have to be at work by eight—and, anyway, he would ask her to telephone the police station and find out in French why they were holding Spinola.

Alec turned on his side and studied Isabelle's features—soft, feminine; long eyelashes, curved lips, rosy skin. He got up at 6:30, quickly showered and dressed, and called room service to order cappucino and croissants.

Isabelle rubbed her eyes. "What happened last night? Where did you go?"

"Remember that man you met in Le Texan?" said Alec. "My associate in the lottery business?"

"Oui," said Isabelle.

"He was arrested last night by the police."

"In Monaco?"

"Yes. But I don't know why. Could you call for me and find out?"

"Of course. What is his name?"

"Gerry Spinola."

Isabelle picked up the phone, called the hotel concierge and spoke in French, then jotted down a number. She dialed, spoke a few words in French and waited. Alec sat nearby, trying to conceal his frayed nerves.

"I'm holding," she whispered to Alec, then turned back to the phone. "Oui," she spoke into the mouthpiece. "Gerry Spinola, Americaine." Another pause. "Isabelle Auriol."

Shit, thought Alec, he didn't want Isabelle's name dragged into this.

"Mon ami," he heard Isabelle say. Another pause. Isabelle hung up and turned to Alec. "They say it is a serious matter. They say I should come to the bureau, police headquarters, in Condamine—they won't talk over the phone."

Alec didn't like the sound of that. But he had to know what was going on and not act rashly; good intelligence was everything. And what could they do to Isabelle? She knew nothing; was guilty of nothing.

"Could you stop by there on the way to work?" Alec asked casually. "See what's going on?"

"Of course. Isabelle phoned the institut and left a message on the answering machine that she might be late.

Alec drove with Isabelle to La Condamine and waited inside the Café Dauphin Verte as Isabelle entered the police station. An hour and fifteen minutes later, Isabelle emerged. She walked briskly to the Dauphin and joined Alec.

"Why were you so long?" asked Alec.

"They made me wait almost one hour. They said it is a serious matter with your friend."

"What has he done?"

"They say they caught him cheating in the gaming room, a serious offense in Monaco. They say they could deport him, not only from the principality, but from the whole riviera. They haven't decided yet."

"What happens next?"

"They're checking with the police in America to see if he has a criminal record, and since Monaco is six hours ahead, they expect him to stay there all day, maybe tonight, too." Isabelle paused. "They also asked who am I."

"What did you say?"

"I said I am a translator for a man involved with Gerry on business. Then they asked which man."

"What did you say?"

"I made up a name and I said the man was staying in Cannes, but had already returned to America."

"Good thinking. I'm sorry to put you through this."

"I think they believe Gerry's business here is gambling, which I guess is true," laughed Isabelle.

"Pardon?"

"The lottery is gambling, isn't it?"

"Yes, of course," said Alec.

Isabelle checked her watch. "I'm very late."

"I'm so sorry," said Alec. "You leave first, just in case they're watching you."

Isabelle looked puzzled. "Why are you so worried?"

"Just naturally cautious," smiled Alec. "The lottery is a funny business."

Isabelle leaned over and the pair kissed. Then Isabelle was off, and Alec waited five minutes before exiting the café. He walked back to Loews at a brisk pace.

There was a message waiting for him at the hotel: "Ted phoned—will call back at 11 a.m." Alec looked at his watch; just past 10:45.

Barry Zubrick called at eleven on the dot. "Where have you been?" he snapped.

"More trouble with The Dentist," said Alec. "This time it's serious."

"Does it effect our plans?"

"It might," said Alec. "We should meet."

"Goddam it," said Barry. "As if I don't have enough to do! All right. The H place in 30 minutes, got it?"

"I'll be there."

Alec waited for Barry outside the Hermitage, in Beaumarchais Square, and when he saw Barry appear at the door of Le Sporting d'Hiver, he waved his hand, signaling him to stop, and crossed the street to join Barry.

"Let's walk," said Alec. "I prefer talking in the open air."

Barry looked up and down the street. "Let's cut back in here."

Alec followed Barry into Le Sporting d'Hiver, past the fine wine shop, with its wines and cognacs dating back to 1905.

"Let's go in here." Barry ushered Alec into the Haagen Daz ice cream parlor and chose a table set back against an inside wall. "I'm being followed," Barry whispered.

"Oh, shit," said Alec. "The police?"

"No, a damn reporter. Bill Blade from the *Miami Herald*."

"What does *he* want with you?"

"It was his damn article that started this whole thing," said Barry. "And now he's come here to dig up dirt on me."

"Where is he?"

"He could be hiding anywhere." Barry looked around nervously. "He's staying at Loews and he staked me out yesterday at the post office, my accommodation address."

Alec shook his head. "The police have The Dentist."

"Holy Maloly! Do they know?"

"I don't think so," said Alec. "If he'd talked, they'd be all over us by now. He was caught cheating at roulette— they're talking about deporting him from Monaco."

"Where is he?"

"Police headquarters in La Condamine. They're holding him till they decide what to do. My concern is that he'll strike a deal with them, tell them about our plans in exchange for his freedom."

"Matsalah!" said Barry. "Do you think he will?"

"I'm saying it's possible—you know what he's like."

"What'll we do?"

"Nothing—wait it out. But there's an up-side to this," said Alec. "If they've got him locked up, he can't get in any more trouble, and we know exactly where to find him when we need him."

"What's the down side?"

"That he spills his guts and they throw us both in jail. And they'd probably throw away the key."

"But we've only got three-and-a-half-days to go," said Barry. "Don't you think he can hold out?"

"Probably not. But short of calling it off and hopping a plane, there's nothing we can do."

"Can we get to him?" asked Barry. "Will they allow him visitors?"

"I don't know," said Alec. "But we sure don't want either of us walking in there, creating suspicion. There's that flaky blond, but she'd only make things worse." Alec suddenly realized he should call Vicky, try to get rid of her before she figured out where Spinola was and tried to go there on her own. God knew what the dentist had already told her. "Let's just carry on business as usual," said Alec. "We can't allow ourselves to get hyped up and nervous—that's when mistakes happen."

"What do I do about that frigging reporter?" asked Barry.

"Nothing," said Alec. "Just ignore him. Remember, he's the one who wants something from *you*, not the other way 'round." Alec thought for a moment. "We might even have a use for him when this thing is over. It would be worthwhile to have an ally in the media. Maybe we'll let him be first to interview the new prince. God knows, that dentist is going to need a friend among the press corps—they're going to tear him to shreds."

"You're right, Alec. Good point."

"What's news from J.J.?"

"Everything's on schedule. He's coming in today."

"Good. At least something's going right."

Barry finished his ice cream, looked up and down Le Sporting d'Hiver, and sprinted through the door.

Alec walked back to Loews, telephoned the Abela Hotel from a public phone in the lobby and asked for Dr. Spinola's room.

"Hello?" said Vicky.

"It's Alec. I've got some news about Gerry."

"Oh, thank God. I've been soooo worried. Where is he?"

"The police are holding him," said Alec. "They say they caught him cheating at roulette. Is that true?"

"The pigs! They're the ones who cheat. They don't let you bet zero or double-zero, what kind of rule is that? Spinny was just evening the score. Poor Spinneeeee. What are they doing to him?"

"They're going to send him back to the States," lied Alec. "The best thing you can do is go back and wait for him."

"When?" whined Vicky.

"Any time. You should leave as soon as possible."

"How? I don't have any dough."

"I'll call Delta and book you on tomorrow morning's flight," said Alec. "There'll be a ticket waiting for you at the desk. Okay?"

"Okay." Vicky was weeping. "This is terrible—my pooooor baby. Are you sure that's what Spinny wants me to do?"

"Yes, he told me so himself," lied Alec. "He wants you to be there for him when he arrives in the States— he might even be on your plane tomorrow."

"Ya think so?" Vicky perked up.

"Maybe—we'll see."

Alec hung up and set to work organizing Isabelle's translations. His report would rationalize the return to power of the Spinolas, the basis for a legal case; and from this he would derive a press release for public dissemination.

"The Principality of Monaco," he began, writing in longhand on a yellow legal pad, "has been returned to the Spinola family, its rightful owners. Seven centuries ago, on January 9, 1297, Francois Grimaldi illegally seized Monaco from Adolpho Spinola.

"Dr. Gerard Spinola of the United States, a descendant of Adolpho Spinola, has rightfully reclaimed the Principality's territory as his property. Prince Spinola intends that the government of Monaco remain intact and operational, and that the Grimaldis be exiled to a country of their choice. Prince Spinola makes no claims to any bank accounts or property the Grimaldi family possesses outside of Monaco, but he takes possession of the Palace and all real estate owned by the Grimaldi family inside the Principality.

"Prince Spinola wishes it to be known that he intends to honor the Monaco Constitution and, in particular, its pact with France."

Alec suddenly remembered SBM, and he looked through Isabelle's notes to see if this had been addressed. Yes, the Société des Bains de la Mer—sea-bathing society—a name devised as a respectable gloss for the unsavory business of gambling when Monaco's first casino opened its doors in the mid-19th century. For many years, SBM was a private company that shared its gambling revenues with the principality and, under the table, with a handful of government officials. It was also charged with underwriting the operation of Monaco's municipal services. In the mid-20th century, it was deemed to be too powerful, and the reigning Grimaldi Prince effectively nationalized SBM, taking control of a majority shareholding. It was murky waters over whether or not the extremely private shareholding was in the name of the Grimaldi, but the official line was that SBM— or, Monaco, Inc.—was controlled by the government.

Alec made a note to advise Barry Zubrick to freeze all SBM accounts as his first executive order and to launch a full investigation of SBM's holdings. He would also need to halt all transactions at the Bourse, the stock exchange in Paris, where a minority holding of SBM was publicly traded. Alec added that a new chairman—someone loyal to Barry—should be appointed immediately.

Alec returned to his report:

"Prince Spinola intends to conduct a comprehensive review of SBM's activities and the every-day business of Monaco. No immediate changes are planned. Foreign residents are encouraged to remain in the Principality..."

Alec scribbled another note for Barry: "All bank accounts should be frozen for one week lest foreign residents panic and transfer their money all at once out of the Principality and bankrupt Monaco's banks—it will take time to convince them that their money will still be safe in Monaco." Alec had already discovered that the real money-spinner in Monaco was money itself. Because of its relaxed tax laws, Monaco's banks and financial institutions attracted money from around the world.

"Prince Spinola regretfully declares a 48-hour curfew. This is to ensure the safety of Monaco's citizens and residents while the Prince negotiates his standing with France. During this time, Monaco's borders will be closed."

Alec re-read what he had written, then lay back on his bed and closed his eyes. What the devil had he gotten himself into?

8

General John J. Stemmer chomped on his unlit cigar as he jumped aboard the Panama-registered S.S. *Monkey House* docked at Menton, a quarter-mile from the Italian border. He beat a path downstairs to the galley to inspect a stack of wooden crates that lined the walls. They were marked "Video Cassettes." J.J. grabbed a crowbar and pried open two of the crates, inspected a sampling of his goods and climbed back upstairs. Two rental vans from Euro Dollar awaited him, their back doors swung open several feet from the gangplank, and eight deck hands quickly loaded the crates onto the vehicles.

J.J. got behind the wheel of his own rented Ford Escort and led the vans in a casual convoy along Menton's beach route to Cap Martin, and up into the mountains to the Vista Palace Hotel. J.J.'s men unloaded the crates into a large storeroom. This was the "audio-visual and translation equipment" J.J. had mentioned to the hotel's manager, for which he was given a key to the storeroom.

Colonel Piers Furnivall arrived soon after with six of his men, and J.J. joined them to take full inventory of the weapons and ammunition: submachine guns, rocket launchers, grenades, stun grenades—the Colonel ticked each item off a master checklist pinned to a clipboard. When they had finished, Furnivall instructed one of his men to install a new padlock on the storeroom door.

J.J. and the Colonel retired to the bar, ordered Ricard, a liquorice flavored pastis from Marseilles, and gazed quietly out the picture windows. In the distance, toward Menton, a group of hang-gliders smoothly descended from a mountain to the sea. J.J. watched and commented on the grace of such a sport.

"My men," said Colonel Furnivall.

"Huh?" J.J. grunted.

"Those are my men. They're practicing."

J.J. smiled in appreciation.

*****

Gerry Spinola sat on a simple wooden chair in a small room, facing a mustachioed police officer, plainclothed, sitting behind a barren desk.

"Your name?" said the officer.

"I already told three of youz guys," said Spinola. "How many times do ya need to know my name?"

The officer looked up briefly, then looked down again at the documents in front of him, and looked up again. "You are in a good deal of trouble—please answer my questions. Your name?"

"I am *Doctor* Gerard Spinola, D.D.S."

"What are you doing in Monaco?"

"I'm a dentist. I came to see a patient."

"All the way from America?"

"Yeah, yeah, patients call me from all over the world."

"Who is your patient?"

"Uh, his name is Barry Zubrick"

"Nationality?"

"Uh, I don't know—American, I think."

"And how long have you known this Barry Zubrick?"

"A few days."

"Only a few days?" The Frenchman raised his eyebrows.

"Uh, yeah—I was recommended to him."

"Yes? By whom?"

"Uh, I don't know."

"You don't know?"

"No, I just got a . . . got a . . . call—to come."

"From Barry Zubrick?"

"Uh, no. From someone else."

"Who?"

Spinola gulped. "Uh, Alec Perry," he said in a low voice.

"Who? Speak up."

"Alec Perry."

"And who is Alec Perry?" asked the French officer.

"I don't know."

"You don't know?"

"He works for Barry Zubrick."

"What kind of work?"

"I don't know."

"You don't know?"

"No."

"American?"

"Who?"

"Alec Perry—American?"

"Yeah, yeah, I think so."

"You think so?"

"Yeah, that's what I just said."

"How long have you known him?"

"Uhhhh, about four days."

"*Four days?*"

"Yeah, four days, maybe five."

"Then you came to Monaco." The police had already pulled Spinola's passport details from the file.

"Yeah, that's right."

"And why did this Alec Perry call you to fix the teeth of Barry Zubrick?"

"How the hell am I supposed to know?" said Spinola. "I'm a dentist. I fix teeth. Why the hell *not* call me?"

"But it seems a long way from New Jersey to fix teeth."

"Go figure," said Spinola. "Maybe he doesn't like French dentists."

"Perhaps not. But there is an American dentist in Monaco."

Spinola shrugged.

"What kind of problem does Barry Zubrick have?"

"Problem?"

"With his teeth."

"I don't know—ask *him*."

"But you are the dentist—you came to look at his teeth."

"He hasn't shown them to me yet."

"Why not?"

"I don't know. He's busy, I guess."

"Monsieur Spinola, this doesn't make any sense to me."

"*Doctor*, to you. I'm sorry if it doesn't make sense to you, but it's not really my problem. Can I leave now?"

"No. It may be your problem. I have more questions. How much money does Monsieur Zubrick pay you to come here and *not* look at his teeth?"

Spinola said nothing.

"Let me re-phrase my question," said the Frenchman. "Why would Monsieur Zubrick pay you thirty-thousand dollars to come to Monaco to fix his teeth and then not show them to you?"

"How do you know that?" shot Spinola. "I mean, what right do you have to pry into my financial affairs. I'm an American. I have rights, ya know!"

"This is Monaco," said the Frenchman. "And you are *here*, not in America. Please answer my question."

"What's the question?" said Spinola.

"Why has Monsieur Zubrick paid you thirty-thousand dollars?"

"I told you—to come over and fix his teeth."

"But you *haven't seen* his teeth."

Spinola leaned back in his chair and rolled his eyes. "It's gonna be real tough to look at *anybody's* teeth stuck in this zoo. I wanna see the American ambassador."

"The American Consulate in Marseilles has been informed of your status."

"What status?"

"Monsieur Spinola, this is a most serious matter."

"What's the matter?"

"We are holding you here while we consider charges. You are suspected of cheating at the roulette table, a grave offense in the principality . . ."

"I *wasn't* cheating! What kind of dogshit is that?"

The French officer stared at the dentist impassively. "Why are you in Monaco, Monsieur Spinola?"

Spinola banged his head three times with his fist. "I wanna see a lawyer—don't I get a lawyer, one phone call? What kinda fascist police state is this anyway?"

The French officer stood up, glared at Spinola and strode out of the room.

"I wanna lawyer!" Spinola hollered; the Frenchman closed the door behind him.

*****

The French detective went to see his supervisor. "Something is not correct," he said. "I want to pick up Alec Perry, bring him in for questioning. He has been seen several times with this 'dentist' Spinola."

"D'accord," grunted the captain.

The detective grabbed a couple of uniformed officers and a marked car and drove to Loews. The uniforms followed the detective into the lobby and up to reception.

"Do you have Monsieur Alec Perry staying here?" he asked.

"We did have. He checked out one hour ago."

The detective raced back to police headquarters and pulled Alec Perry's registration details from the hotel-linked computer. It listed his nationality as "USA" and his address as "P.O. Box 684, Glen Echo, MD, USA."

*****

By instinct—a spy's instinct—Alec Perry had decided the time had come to leave Loews; to leave Monaco. He knew it was possible the Monaco police would try to question him because of his association with Spinola— mostly because Spinola's room at Loews had been in Alec's name. And, in case he was being followed, Alec did not want to risk leading the police to the Vista Palace Hotel, operational headquarters. So he took a taxi to the train station at Nice, waited ten minutes over a cappucino, then grabbed a taxi back to Rocquebrune, the other side of Monaco, and checked into Les Deux Frères, the small, cheerful inn whose fireplace he had so enjoyed with Isabelle on their first night together.

Alec checked in under an assumed name—Jason Meade—for which he always kept a driver's license, American Express charge card and a library card.

After having dinner in the restaurant, Alec had the hotel call a taxi and he rode the short ride along the Moyen Corniche to the Vista Palace Hotel. General Stemmer and Colonel Furnivall were expecting him, and they met in J.J.'s suite. The general turned on the TV softly to muffle any sound. It was unlikely they were being bugged, but J.J. took no chances.

"Everything is in place," said J.J., unlit cigar in mouth. "Weapons are here—so is more than half our force. Colonel?"

Colonel Piers Furnivall's stiff upper lip was framed with a wiry moustache, its thick hairs pointing straight out, closely clipped not to go beyond the edges of his mouth. His posture was ram-rod military and he spoke in abrupt bursts, strong on enunciation.

"Twenty-two men are here," said the colonel. "Rehearsals are underway. Thirteen men still to arrive, this evening and tomorrow."

"And your end Alec?" asked J.J.

"Remember the weakest link I was talking about?"

J.J. grunted.

"It just snapped."

J.J. grabbed the cigar out of his mouth and thumped it on the table. "What the hell are you talking about, Alec?"

"The Dentist. Spinola. The police have him."

J.J. looked dumbfounded. He glanced at Colonel Furnivall and looked back at Alec.

"I packed him off to Nice, but he came back, re-
turned to the casino and was apparently caught cheating.
They've been holding him since early this morning"—
Alec looked at his watch—"about 18 hours."

"Does Barry know?"

"Yes. We met this morning. He's having problems of
his own with a pesky reporter."

"Bloody hell," said Colonel Furnivall. "Trust you
yanks for a balls-up."

"Let's stay in control here," said J.J. "Alec, what's
your assessment?"

"I think we have to assume Spinola will eventually
spill his guts. He goes for quick-cash deals—if they throw
him a bone he'll sit up and do tricks."

"Then we might as well pack our bloody bags and
go home," said Colonel Furnivall.

"Hold on, hold on," said J.J. "How much does the
dentist know?"

"He knows the concept," said Alec. "He doesn't know
timeframe or operational details."

"But if he knows concept and tells them," said Colonel
Furnivall, "they may mobilize and we'll lose the element of
surprise. It'll be a bloody mess with loads of casualties."

"Wait a minute," said J.J. "Do you think they'd really believe him and act so swiftly?"

"I don't think so." J.J. answered his own question.
"We've got to proceed as planned, with one change. We
should do it tomorrow night, Friday, instead of Saturday
night. Do you see any problem with that, colonel?"

"It'll be rushed. But if we're going to move, let's not
lose the element of surprise. It would be desirable,"
Furnivall added, "not to have to take on the bloody French
army."

"Then that's what we'll do," said J.J., stuffing his cigar back into his mouth. He checked his watch; it was now past 9:15. "Where the hell is Barry?" asked J.J. "He was supposed to be here at nine. That pecksniff is *never* late."

"Do *you* have his phone number?" asked Alec.

"Are you kidding? I don't think his *mother* knows how to call him."

Alec suppressed a laugh. He had an uneasy feeling about Barry's absence. "Do you know where he lives? Or is that another stupid question?"

J.J. closed his eyes and puffed on his unlit cigar.

By 10:30 and no Barry Zubrick, Alec began to fear the worst.

*****

The French detective had quickly located the Monagasque taxi driver who picked up Alec Perry outside Loews. The detective could only guess that Alec had taken the night train to Paris, or elsewhere. Faced with Alec's disappearance, he had gone to his captain with a new plan.

"I would like to bring Barry Zubrick in for questioning. This dentist Spinola can work on his teeth," he grinned sardonically.

"Monsieur Zubrick is a resident," said the captain. "Are you sure this is necessary?"

"Yes," said the detective.

"Let me first consult Monsieur Zubrick's file." He picked up the phone and dialed the Bureau d'Etranger on another floor. The captain spoke a few words, listened, and put down the phone, a bewildered expression on his face. "The residency of Monsieur Zubrick has been terminated. He has been ordered to leave the principality and has only ten days left."

"Does that mean I can bring him in?"

*****

Barry Zubrick was sitting in his home-office, studying a sudden rise in the price of gold, when the buzzer rang, indicating that someone was downstairs. The only person who ever came to Barry's home was the Filipino maid, but she wasn't expected at 7:15 this evening.

He picked up the intercom phone apprehensively. "Hello?"

"Ah, Monsieur Zubrick? Is zee concierge. Zee polizia want to see you."

Barry verged on panic. He looked around, thinking fast. There was no escape—and he sure as hell didn't want them up in his apartment. Wait a minute, there was the back elevator to the basement parking levels.

"I'll come down," said Barry.

Barry pulled on a sport coat and descended to the second level of the basement. It was dark—the light switches were connected to timers to save electricity—and Barry liked it that way. He snuck around a corner, then up to level minus-one, around another corner, and he could see light coming down the car ramp, the garage exit. Barry walked to the exit, glanced up and down the street, and made a run for it.

Barry got about 50 yards before the police pounced on him. Two uniformed officers and one plain-clothed detective.

"Going somewhere, Monsieur Zubrick?" asked the detective.

"Yes, what do you want?" said Barry.

"We need to ask you a few questions. Will you come with us?"

"Ask them here. I'm busy."

"No, Monsieur Zubrick. We prefer for you to come with us."

"Are you arresting me?" asked Barry.

"No, we wish for you to answer our questions."

"Then I'll talk to you later." Barry started to walk away.

The detective signaled the uniformed officers and they sprang to action, sandwiching Barry between them, restraining his arms. They marched him down the street and into the back seat of their car.

"This is an outrage!" screamed Barry. "If you're arresting me, say so—or let me go!"

The officers ignored his protests and, once inside the car, Barry turned quiet; the car remained silent throughout the short ride to police headquarters in La Condamine.

Barry was flushed with rage as he was paraded into the police building and taken to an interrogation room by the uniformed officers, who left him there alone. Minutes later, he was joined by the detective, who sat in a chair, behind a desk.

"Do you know a man named Gerry Spinola?" asked the detective.

Barry didn't answer.

"I am asking, do you know a man named Gerry Spinola?"

"I refuse to answer any questions until my lawyer is here. His name is Alan Bennett and he works at Bennett & Bergonzi."

"Do you know a man named Gerry Spinola?"

"I will not answer one question until my lawyer is here," snapped Barry.

"Monsieur Zubrick," said the detective, "if you don't cooperate with me, I may be forced to freeze your bank accounts in the principality."

"You can't do that!" yelled Barry.

"There is a lot I can do, Monsieur Zubrick. I can put you on a plane and send you back to the United States. Would you like that?"

Barry shuddered.

"I just want to know if you know a man named Gerry Spinola?"

"Why *should* I know him?" snapped Barry.

"I just want to know if you *do?*"

"No. Doesn't ring a bell."

"No? He says he knows you."

"Who knows me?"

"Gerry Spinola."

"Let me think." Barry paused. "Oh, is he a dentist?"

The detective said nothing, sat poker-faced.

"Yeah," said Barry. "Maybe he's the dentist I sent for."

"I see," said the detective. "Do you have a problem with your teeth?"

"As a matter of fact, I do," snapped Barry. "But I hardly see how that has anything to do with you."

"Why do you bring a dentist all the way from America?"

"It is against your laws for me to bring my own dentist to Monaco for private treatment?"

"I want to know *why?*"

"I am a wealthy man," said Barry. "And I assume— or I did until thirty minutes ago—that I am free to spend my money any way I choose."

"But we have many good dentists in Monaco," said the detective.

"I prefer an American dentist."

"We have an American dentist."

"Him? He's been here so long he's as *good* as French."

The detective ignored the slight.

"What actually is wrong with your mouth?" asked the detective.

"This is getting ridiculous," snapped Barry. "Is it possible my *mouth* is breaking Monaco's laws?"

"This is a serious matter. We have arrested Monsieur Spinola."

"For what?"

"Never mind for the moment." The detective paused briefly. "Why did you give Monsieur Spinola thirty-thousand dollars?"

"What?" Barry gulped.

"Why did you give Gerry Spinola thirty-thousand dollars?"

"Partly to cover his expenses and partly to pay for the extensive work on my teeth."

The detective wrote this down. "And who," he asked, "is Alec Perry?"

"Who?" asked Barry.

"Alec Perry of Maryland, USA. Do you know him?"

"Should I know him, too?"

"I think so."

"Why? Who is Alec Perry?"

"That's what I want you to tell me."

"No." Barry shook his head. "I don't know any Alec Perry."

"Let me tell you what I think," said the detective. "I think that you are involved in a conspiracy with Monsieur Spinola and Monsieur Perry to cheat the casino of

Monte Carlo. That is why you brought him here, and that is why you gave him thirty-thousand dollars."

"Bollocks!" said Barry. "That's the most ridiculous thing I've ever heard. I am a multi-millionaire. Why do I need to cheat your casino? I *hate* casinos!"

"Nonetheless, Monsieur Zubrick, I can charge you with conspiracy to defraud the Principality of Monaco."

"If that's what you're going to do, then do it," barked Barry. "But I'm not saying another word until my lawyer Bennett is here."

9

Colonel Furnivall went over the plan one last time in a locked and guarded convention room at the Vista Palace Hotel.

There were seven teams, each with a different target and agenda, and the colonel dealt with each. He asked that everyone synchronize their watches: it was 7:12 p.m., less than five hours until commencement.

At midnight, Team A, eight men, including Colonel Furnivall, climbed into a van loaded with their equipment. They drove slowly up to the Grand Corniche and along the narrow, badly-lit road to the Tete de Chien, high above La Condamine and the Rock.

Team B, another eight men, jumped into a second van and cruised the winding roads down to the principality, into La Condamine, where they parked on the corner of Rue Suffren Reymond and Boulevard Prince Albert 1st, outside the Sûreté Publique building, police headquarters.

Team C, two men, departed an hour earlier. They were now on board the *S.S. Monkey House*, lifting anchor from Menton.

Team D, four men, drove in a Renault Five, to Boulevard Princesse Charlotte in Monte Carlo, parked and waited.

Team E, six men, divided into groups of two, drove mini-buses to Monaco's three main points of entry: on the east side, at St. Roman; on the west side, on the Basse Corniche at Cap d'Ail, and on the Moyen Corniche at Jardin Exotique.

Team F, two men dressed fashionably in sport coats and ties, drove to the Sporting d'Eté, parked, and walked into Jimmy'z Discotech. They were shown to a table near the dance floor, and they ordered Coca-Colas, at 240 francs, 40 dollars, the most expensive cokes of their lives.

Team G, two two-man teams, set out in small cars for Monaco's train station and the heliport in Fontvieille, to be joined later by two helicopter pilots.

At the Vista Palace Hotel, General Stemmer and Alec Perry sat inside the bar, sipping Coca-Cola and watching Monaco through the floor-to-ceiling plate glass window. Alec glanced at his watch: five to one.

*****

The men at Jimmy'z checked their watches. At 1 a.m. they beckoned a waiter's attention. He was quickly at their table.

"Anuzzer round?"

Both Brits stood up. "Are you bonkers?" shouted one of them. "We're not paying fifty quid for two Cokes."

"Ah, but you must pay." The waiter stood his ground.

"Get lost!" said the Brit. He pushed the waiter and both he and the drinks he was carrying tumbled around him, onto the floor, splashing three young Italian men and their dates.

The men rose, yelling in Italian, pulling off their jackets for a fight, and the Brits picked up several chairs and crashed them onto nearby tables. Fists flew, to the strains of "I Will Survive," and the dance-floor became a battle zone beneath pulsating flourescent black light.

From the Vista Palace, J.J. and Alec watched a convoy of flashing blue police lights racing along the beachfront to Jimmy'z.

Simultaneously, eight men in wetsuits, blackened faces and black hang-gliders, launched themselves from the Tete de Chien into the moonless sky. They gently steered themselves down, gliding with ease into the back garden of the palace, carefully avoiding the olive trees and the swimming pool. Silently, they stormed Carabinieri headquarters on the ground floor, made prisoners of the six guards on duty and secured the palace grounds. One of Furnivall's men dressed into the white uniform of the Carabinieri and replaced the sole guard at the front of the palace.

Down below, in La Condamine, the van carrying Team B pulled up alongside the entrance to police headquarters. Eight men jumped out the back and stormed the Sûreté Publique.

A French policeman near the door tried to pull a pistol from his holster, but only got as far as unlatching the leather strap. A burst of gunfire left him slumped on the ground, bleeding profusely from a leg wound. Other police officers, witnessing the scene, raised their hands in horror. Most of the officers on duty had driven to Jimmy'z to deal with the a disturbance that had been reported minutes earlier—Stemmer's diversion. It took only minutes to secure the police building and take control of its operations command post. Four men remained up front. Four others, in teams of two, searched the building, using the stairs, floor by floor.

The four men on Avenue Princess Charlotte raced

into the offices of Radio Monte Carlo and commandeered
the control room. Radio Monte Carlo's skeleton crew
were rounded up and locked in a storage room. Two of
Furnivall's men guarded the front entrance, a third took
position at the controls and a fourth sat at the announcer's
desk. He unbuckled his leather satchel and spread a sheaf
of papers in front of him.

Out upon the water, two men aboard the *S.S. Monkey
House* laid a dozen mines along the entrance to
Monaco's port, between the pair of lighthouses on
Monaco's two stone jetties, then whizzed around the Rock
to Fontvieille and laid a second series of mines blocking
the sea entrance to the quiet Monaco suburb.

And at Monaco's three main border points, six men
of Team E neutralized the single police officer on duty at
each point and erected roadblocks with their mini-buses.

Two men from Team A, the palace, raced to the top
of the only road that ascends the Rock, blocked it with
three limousines from the palace fleet and set up grenade
launchers.

By 1:30 a.m., the principality was effectively under
the control of Colonel Piers Furnivall, who now sat inside
the contemporary Great Salon in the Prince of Monaco's
private apartment.

Furnivall turned on his mobile phone and pressed a
few numbers, connecting him with J.J. at the Vista Palace.

"We are home," said Colonel Furnivall. "Do join us
for tea."

As J.J. and Alec negotiated the winding roads from
the Vista Palace down to Monaco, Furnivall dispatched
two of his men to waken the minister of state, a Frenchman, whose villa was but a hundred yards from the palace.

A police van carrying the two Brits from Jimmy'z

was greeted at the front entrance of police headquarter's by two of their compatriots, who sprang out with Kalishnikovs and turned the tables on the four shocked French police officers.

"Thanks for the ride, mate!" winked one of the Brits. The officers were shepherded into the building, locked into a room with their colleagues, and the same treatment was given to other policemen as they returned from Jimmy'z in dribs and drabs.

J.J. and Alec were waved through the St. Roman roadblock and continued on to police headquarters in La Condamine. The pair marched into the building.

"Good work," said J.J. to Team B's commander. "Have you found Barry Zubrick and the dentist?"

"Not yet. My men are still searching."

"Alec! How ya doin'!" At the far end of a corridor, Gerry Spinola appeared, rubbing his eyes. "Shee-it, I need a good stiff drink!"

Then Barry Zubrick appeared, from another direction, disheveled, unsmiling.

"What's going on?" he snapped. "I wasn't expecting you till *tomorrow* night."

"Couldn't take any chances," said J.J. "We couldn't be sure of what they knew."

"Well they sure as hell didn't get anything out of me." Barry threw an irritated glance at Spinola, then looked around. "Where are the police?"

"We've got them all in there," said Team B's commander pointing to a closed door.

"I wanna see them," said Barry. "Open the door."

"Why?" asked J.J.

"Just open the damn door!"

Team B's commander unlocked the door with a key,

opened it for Barry, who peeked inside, saw the officers sitting around, then took a step forward. He recognized a few faces from his arrest.

"You, you and you," snapped Barry. "You're fired!" The officers looked at each other in bewilderment.

Barry stepped out and the commander re-locked the door.

"Is this it?" Spinola brightened. "Am I *prince* now?"

Barry shot a look of disgust at Spinola. "Don't get any big ideas, sonny. *I'm* in charge now. But as far as these frogs are concerned, you're officially Prince Spinola."

"That means I get a million bucks?"

"Not so fast," said Alec. "It's not over yet. C'mon, let's get over to the palace."

J.J., Barry, Alec and Spinola spilled out of the building and into the car, drove the wrong way up Rue Suffren Reymond, hung a left onto Rue Grimaldi and, at the Place des Armes, the intersection at the Rock, a lone uniformed policeman raised his hand and blew a whistle. Only cars with Monegasque tags were allowed to ascend the Rock. J.J.'s Peugeot, rented at Nice airport, sported French tags.

The white-gloved police officer bent over, saluted as was customary and spoke rapidly in French, his manner suggesting he was delivering a reprimand.

J.J. raised a pistol he had rested on his lap and pointed it between the officer's eyes. Alec got out the other side, opened the back trunk and gestured that the officer climb inside, which he did, a stern, indignant expression on his face.

The car continued up the Rock, lights flashing several times to signal the roadblock at the top, which waved them through. Past the Ministre d'Etat building, the local school, St. Maur, and on to the faded pink palace at the far end. They were saluted by their own white-uniformed Carabinieri, now on duty, and welcomed inside the palace car park by Team A's commander, who led them to the prince's private apartment.

Colonel Furnivall was sitting with Jean-Pierre Grazin, the French minister of state, who had not yet been told what was going on; only that he should wait.

"May I introduce Prince Spinola." Colonel Furnivall stood to attention. "He has arrived this morning to reclaim his principality."

Spinola thrust out his hand to the minister of state, who had remained seated. "Gerry Spinola. Good to meet ya."

Jean-Pierre recoiled in horror; did not offer his own hand. "What is the meaning of this?" said Jean-Pierre, facing Colonel Furnivall.

"At ease, colonel, I'll take over," said J.J. He faced Jean-Pierre. "I am General Stemmer. This is Alec Perry. And this is Prince Spinola. We are in control of the principality."

"But, but you can't do this," Jean-Pierre sputtered.

"We *have* done this," said J.J. "I am temporarily in command. Monaco is under martial law until a smooth transfer can take place."

"This is impossible," said Jean-Pierre. "My government will never allow this."

"I think they will," said J.J. "After some negotiation."

Jean-Pierre folded his arms. "I cannot negotiate with you. I do not recognize your authority."

"I appreciate your position," said J.J. "You must receive your instructions from Paris. I suggest that you call the Elysées Palace and speak with the president."

"At this hour?"

"This is no practical joke," said J.J. "He should know about this *now*." J.J. handed the minister of state a telephone.

Jean-Pierre knew the number by heart; he and the president had studied politics together at the Sorbonne, were old friends.

"Jacques? Jean-Pierre Grazin. Sorry to wake you. You aren't going to believe this. There has been a coup d'état in Monaco."

Jean-Pierre paused as President Jacques Ducruet spoke.

"No, I'm serious," said Jean-Pierre. "A coup. Americans. I am with them now, at the palace . . ."

J.J. grabbed the telephone. "Mr. President? This is General John Stemmer. I am working at the command of Prince Spinola, not as a representative of the Uni . . ."

"*Quoi? Quoi?* . . ." said Jacques Ducruet.

"You're wasting your time," said Jean-Pierre. "The president does not speak English."

"Tell him for me," said J.J., handing Jean-Pierre the phone. "Tell him the United States is not involved in this action. We have acted to return the Principality of Monaco to the Spinola family, its rightful owners."

Jean-Pierre spoke into the phone, listened and turned to J.J. "The president says you are crazy."

"Please tell the president that we may be crazy," said J.J., "but we are also militarily in command of the principality."

Jean-Pierre, again, spoke into the phone, then listened. "The president says if this is true, you must surrender."

"Tell the President," said J.J., "we have no intention

of surrendering. We have no ill-will toward France and, in fact, we are willing to set conditions that are favorable to France in order to secure a peaceful coexistence with France."

Jean-Pierre talked into the phone, paused, answered several questions and hung up.

"What happened?" said J.J.

"The president continues to insist that you are nuts. But he says he wishes to check on a few things, then call me back."

"Damn frogs," barked Barry. "Don't even trust each other!"

The minister diplomatically pretended not to hear.

The telephone rang, answered by the minister, who listened, then faced J.J. and spoke. "The president says he has spoken with the Prince of Monaco at Roc Agel and that everything seems in order. He thinks I am playing a practical joke on him."

Just then, a second phone rang, on an antique table near Barry Zubrick. Barry answered and listened to a barrage of French smack him in the ear. The only words he could decipher were *"Prince de Monaco."*

"It's for the Prince of Monaco," said Barry, gesturing to Spinola to take the phone.

"Me?" asked Spinola.

"Well, you're the goddam *prince* now," said Barry. "Who else?"

Spinola meekly took the phone. "Doc . . . uh, Prince Spinola, Prince of Monaco."

The man on the other end now spoke English. Spinola turned white as he listened, and put his hand over the mouthpiece. "He says he's the Prince of Monaco," said Spinola. "What should I say?"

"Tell him he *used to be*," barked Barry.

"No, wait, put Jean-Pierre on the phone," said J.J.

The minister was still trying to convince the French president that he was not playing a joke.

"The Prince of Monaco is on the phone," J.J. interrupted.

"Former!" snapped Barry.

Jean-Pierre told President Ducruet to hold on. He put down the receiver and walked to the other telephone. "Your Serene Highness," said Jean-Pierre. "I regret to inform you that there appears to have been a coup d'état in your principality." He listened. "No, I wouldn't advise that. It is best to remain where you are. I will personally keep you informed."

Jean-Pierre walked back to the other phone. The president had hung up. Jean-Pierre replaced the phone to its cradle, and within seconds it rang. The minister picked it up, listened.

"Ah, now we're getting somewhere," Jean-Pierre whispered to J.J., covering the mouthpiece with his hand. "The Prince of Monaco telephoned the president."

"Former!" snapped Barry.

Jean-Pierre grabbed a pad of paper, scribbled notes as he listened to President Ducruet, then faced J.J.

"The President says you have committed an act of craziness, an illegal occupation. He demands that you surrender immediately, without conditions. And he says that if you do not, France will be compelled to use its military power to remove you by force."

"Mister Minister," said J.J. "We have mined Monaco's two ports. We have fortified the Rock. We are an extremely well-equipped fighting force, and there are over 30,000 people inside the principality. If France attacks, there will be terrible bloodshed. We believe what we have done is legal, and we intend to take our case to the International Court at The Hague. We will not budge. We will defend our principality against all invaders. But we *are* willing to negotiate with France . . ."

Jean-Pierre held up his hand. "Hold on," he said, and he spoke into the phone in French, translating J.J.'s stance. He listened, turned back to J.J. "Negotiation is an impossibility."

"Tell him," said J.J. "Tell him we know about the Hades Covenant."

"What?" said Jean-Pierre.

"The Hades Covenant. Tell him we know all about it."

Jean-Pierre passed on J.J.'s message. It was met with a vacuum of silence on the other end.

"Are you there," asked Jean Pierre, after 20 seconds. "Mister President?" Jean-Pierre listened, his face expressed amazement, and he put the telephone back into its cradle. "President Ducruet is coming to Monaco this morning, maybe by seven. He is bringing his personal bodyguard detachment, that is all." He shook his head in disbelief. "*What* is the Hades Covenant?"

J.J. ignored the question. "Okay, we're off to a good start." He tapped his thick cigar on a coffee table. "Alec?"

"We're scheduled to go on the air at 6 a.m." Alec checked his watch. "In three hours. Simultaneously, we will telephone CNN in Atlanta and give them a full report, focusing on the justification of our actions. We'll also dispatch faxes to the United Nations and the International Court."

"One question for youz guys," said Spinola. "Am I gonna get out of here alive?" He punctuated the question with three staccato farts. "Sorry. I gotta nervous stomach. Anyone got any Brioschi?"

"Isn't there something you can go to make him more princely?" barked Barry.

"C'mon," said Alec, to Spinola. "Let's take a look around the royal closets. It's probably too late for elocution lessons, but maybe we can make you *look* presentable."

The minister of state shook his head.

As a pink sun cast first light on the Tete de Chien, the only visible sign of the coup's effect on Monaco was traffic, piling up at the eastern border. Italians from San Remo, Bordighera and Ventimighlia commuted to Monaco each morning—they were the labor force that serviced Monaco's residents: the construction workers, the waiters, the hotel chambermaids. And none of them were being allowed entry, causing traffic to snarl up in a standstill all the way back to the Italian border five miles away, a cacophony of horn-blowing and mounting tempers. As J.J. had anticipated, the pile-up had the added benefit of fully blockading the eastern border.

Trains from both directions were piled up outside Monaco; they could not pass because Colonel Furnivall's Team G commandos had seized two night trains and disengaged them on the tracks at Monaco's railroad station in La Condamine.

The helicopters at Monaco's heliport in Fontvieille were not flying their regular shuttle to Nice airport; regular flight crews were turned around and sent home as they appeared for work. The choppers had been converted by Furnivall's men to warships, and now they patrolled the skies, inspecting border points, monitoring traffic pile-ups and enforcing a curfew that had just been announced over Radio Monte Carlo.

The first announcement was broadcast at 6 a.m.:

> The Principality of Monaco is in a state if emergency. A 48-hour curfew has been declared by the Prince Sovereign and it is requested that everyone stay indoors. Monaco's borders are temporarily closed. Please do not try to leave the principality. More information will follow later in the day.

That was all, broadcast alternately in French, Italian and English. Many foreign residents hearing the announcement were convinced that the prince was about to declare the introduction of an income tax and that he had closed-off Monaco, frozen everything, to prevent a mass exodus of funds. Native Monegasques initially suspected that the Prince Sovereign had died and that a power struggle was ensuing within the family. Mourning flags began to appear outside many windows.

The open-air food market at Place des Armes, which did not even close on Christmas Day, was silent, empty, as the country farmers who trucked down from the mountains early each morning sat in their vehicles, held up at the border.

Just past seven, a single helicopter appeared on the horizon, whirling in over the sea from the west. Its pilot identified the craft to Fontvieille's control tower as carrying Jacques Ducruet, the President of France. A helicopter was dispatched to greet the chopper and escort it the last half-mile to Fontvieille.

Upon landing, the President's two bodyguards were relieved of their firearms, and the three men were whisked in a van out of Fontvieille and up the Rock, to the Princes'

Palace. The streets were quiet. Many faces appeared at Monaco Ville windows as the van was waved through, into the palace car park.

President Ducruet was led to the private apartments and into the Great Salon where Jean-Pierre Grazin, J.J., Colonel Furnivall and Alec Perry waited. J.J. was puffing furiously on his fat, unlit cigar.

Jean-Pierre made the introductions in French and English. President Ducruet was curt, matter of fact, and spoke through Jean-Pierre.

"Who mentioned the Hades Covenant?" he demanded to know.

"That would be me." J.J. removed the cigar from his lips and exhaled a mouthful of air.

"And what do you know of the Hades Covenant?"

"I know everything about it."

"And what are you proposing to do with such information?" The President's jaw was tight, toughening the slight, lightweight image he presented with his large, tortoise-shell eyeglasses.

"We'll get to that." J.J. spoke slowly, deliberately. "Right now we want to talk about Monaco, negotiate a peaceful co-existence with France."

"Monaco already has a peaceful coexistence with France," snapped Ducruet.

"I'm talking about the new Monaco," said J.J. "Prince Spinola's Monaco."

"There is no such thing," said the President. "It cannot be. You are deluding yourselves."

"We are serious, Mister President. There will be much bloodshed if France tries to intervene."

"I am *more* serious," said President Ducruet. "We cannot, we *will* not permit you to take control of the principality. We are committed to defending the sovereign rule of the prince."

"You must listen to our terms," said J.J. "You might like them."

"It makes no difference what your terms are. You are terrorists. France will not deal with terrorists."

"We are *not* terrorists." J.J. shoved the cigar back into his mouth, letting it jiggle out the corner of his lips as he spoke. "We have recovered property that belongs to the Spinola family. It was *stolen* from them—and even the history books testify to that."

"If you are not terrorists, you are mercenaries," huffed the president. "Whatever may have once been owned by someone else is irrelevant. France recognizes the Prince Sovereign as the rightful ruler of Monaco—it is *you* who are trying to steal."

"Now just calm down," said J.J. "Let's cut the official bullshit and get down to the nitty-gritty. Whether you like it or now, we've got a valid claim. What's more, we're in control, and we have a saying in the United States—'possession is nine-tenths of the law'. In the interest of fair play, we are willing to make a deal that will be beneficial to France—a better deal than it had before."

"But of course," said the president, his sarcasm lost in the translation. "What else would I expect."

"We're not asking for your permission or your blessing," said J.J. "We have taken Monaco and we aim to keep it—or die trying to defend it. We only wish to be pragmatic. And then there's the Hades Covenant."

"I see," said the president. "Is that your tactic, blackmail?"

"Let's just call it a 'basis of understanding'."

"And what is it I am to understand?"

"Understand, Mister President, that if you choose to go to war with the Principality of Monaco, we will use every weapon at our disposal to fight back. I assure you, it will serve the interests of France—and your government, I might add—to negotiate with us, at least listen to what we are offering."

The telephones had been ringing all morning, but now there was a call from Roc Agel that demanded the President Ducruet's attention.

"This is the Prince Sovereign of Monaco," said a voice over the wire in French. "What the hell are you doing there? Why aren't you sending the goddam army, navy and air force in? Is the world going crazy?"

"Please, your Serene Highness," said the president. "I have just arrived and I am dealing with this situation the very best way I know how. I understand your irritation . . ."

"You don't understand shit!" yelled the voice. "You have a responsibility to protect my sovereign rule. Don't fucking procrastinate! Defend my principality you stupid moron!"

The President was growing annoyed, unaccustomed as he was to taking abuse from anyone, let alone this pompous prince.

"Now see here . . ." said President Ducruet.

"No, *you* see here," the voice interjected. "I've had enough of this bullshit. You never learned how to deal with bandits, you weak mutherfucker. I'll personally have your head on a silver platter." The telephone clicked and the voice was gone.

President Ducruet was dumbfounded. He couldn't know that the voice that just scolded him belonged to a former colleague of Alec Perry, not from Roc Agel, but from Paris.

Ducruet turned back to J.J., trembling with rage, momentarily disoriented as he collected his thoughts.

"Can you and I speak privately?" the president asked J.J.

J.J. nodded. He and Ducruet walked to the Small Salon, a den, accompanied by Jean-Pierre, who was needed to translate. They sat down.

"Let me be clear in my head about this situation," said the president. "What exactly do you know about the Hades Covenant?"

"I'll lay it out for you," said J.J. "I don't want you to call my bluff, because there is no bluff. Everyone will suffer if we cannot resolve our little problem here." J.J. took the cigar from his mouth, plunked it on a side table next to his chair. "As you know, Mister President, the Hades Covenant is a secret pact made between your country and Britain, signed by both premiers, both foreign ministers, both defense ministers and the intelligence chiefs at MI6 and SDECE." He paused while his words were translated by Jean-Pierre. "Your countries have agreed to jointly monitor Germany for any sign that she might one day attempt to build a military machine. And you have agreed to jointly attack Germany, bomb its industrial facilities, at the first hint that they are developing nuclear weapons. And France has pledged, as a first line of offense, to use its short-range nuclear missile—the Hades missile— to wipe out German plants."

President Ducruet leaned back on the low sofa, closed his eyes, re-opened them, studied J.J. as the general picked up his cigar and shoved it back between his teeth.

There was a knock at the door. One of the French bodyguards announced that the Prince of Monaco was on the telephone, demanding to speak with President Ducruet.

"Tell him I'm busy," growled the president.

J.J. took the unlit cigar from his mouth, held it between his forefinger and index finger. "Do you want to hear more?" he asked.

Ducruet nodded.

"The reason you were so cooperative with the British was because the British MI6 was blackmailing you. So you are intimately familiar with blackmail, aren't you, Mister President? And do you want to know *how* they were blackmailing you?"

Ducruet held up his hand, "Arrêté, arrêté!"

"Stop," Jean-Pierre translated.

Ducruet turned to Jean-Pierre. "Before we continue, I must have your pledge of secrecy on this matter."

"Yes, Jacques, you have it," said Jean-Pierre.

Ducruet turned back to J.J. and gestured him to continue speaking.

"Because they managed to acquire a bunch of KGB files from World War II. And, according to those files, Mr. President, your father helped Nazi war criminals escape from France at the end of the war."

As Jean-Pierre translated, Ducruet's face flushed. He looked ready to explode, but caught himself, sagged deeper into the sofa.

"You are aware," said J.J. "that if word of the Hades Covenant leaks out, Germany will go nuts, European unity will be a joke—it'll probably disintegrate. And this is quite apart from your own personal consideration. You will be ridiculed in the press. Your political career will be finished. And this is why," continued J.J., "I think you should listen to what we, the rightful owners of Monaco, are willing to offer your government for official acceptance."

"Go on," said Ducruet.

"Right now Monaco shares all tax revenues with France evenly, 50-50. We are willing to change this to 55-45 in your favor. Plus," J.J. continued, "we are willing to give you, personally, one percent out of *our* share which, I assume, you will share with the minister of state, Jean-Pierre."

As he translated, Jean-Pierre did all he could to repress a smile of appreciation.

"Point Two," said J.J. "We propose a new income tax for foreign residents. A straight five percent of all income across the board. We propose the same split with France.

"Point Three: as currently written, Monaco's treaty with France states that the principality reverts to French rule if or when the royal family can no longer provide direct heirs. We offer that France may exercise an option in the year 2099 to annex of the principality and make it part of France."

"That's it," said J.J. "It is an excellent deal for France. And for you."

President Ducruet folded his arms and glared at J.J. "It is a lie about my father," he said.

"The truth of 50 years ago is often a hazy affair," said J.J. He held up a manilla file, handed it to Ducruet, who opened the file and studied the sheaf of looseleaf papers. They were typed in Cyrillic; neither Ducruet nor Jean-Pierre could understand Russian. "Direct from KGB files," said J.J. The papers, prepared by Alec, were actually instructions on how to assemble the Lada, a Russian car, faxed to Alec by a former colleague in Washington. "I am prepared to pass this file onto an investigative reporter here in town—Bill Blade of the *Miami Herald*—

who will be eager to print what for him will be the scoop of a lifetime.

"And, of course," said J.J. "There is also the Hades Covenant. Would you like a little time on your own to think about my offer, Mister President?"

Ducruet said yes; asked to be left alone with Jean-Pierre. J.J. retreated back into the Great Salon.

Day had truly broken; telephones were ringing even more madly than before. Colonel Furnivall was in constant contact with his men, from border points to heliport to police headquarters to both seaports. Someone in a large yacht had attempted to pull anchor and set sail out of Monaco's Hercules Port in La Condamine. It ignored warnings and hit a mine; and now it was burning, sinking into the sea, terrifying other yachtsmen into submission. The western border points, on both the Basse and Moyen Corniches, were backed up six miles to Eze. Horns blared; tempers flared, and one of Furnivall's men had fired a Kalishnikov into the air to keep the peace. Small boats had begun to gather outside Monaco's harbors to see what was going on. They were kept at a fair distance by Furnivall's men, who patrolled the sea in two cigarette speedboats they had commandeered.

Monaco's residents stayed indoors, unsure of what was happening around them, tuning into Radio Monte Carlo and the BBC World Service.

By 6 a.m., as scheduled, Alec Perry had faxed their declaration to the United Nations in New York, the International Court at the Hague and to CNN headquarters in Atlanta. By seven the first news reports began to filter out, the major news organizations treating the story as a humorous aside to the morning's news on Easter weekend. Nobody took Monaco seriously; it was perceived as a Disneyland for adults, a haven for casino gambling and the very rich. So the notion of a coup did not cause outrage, but bemusement among the world's media.

"It is reported," announced CNN, "that a coup d'état has taken place in Monte Carlo, one of the world's glamour spots. Reports coming into CNN suggest that a rival Mediterranean family has laid claim to the principality, known as a paradise to the rich and famous."

This is what Bill Blade heard when he awoke and switched on CNN in his room at Loews. He had been planning to depart that morning, aboard Delta's late morning flight to New York. Blade clicked into gear, showered, dressed and rushed downstairs to the lobby, now filled with tourists who wondered what the hell was going on. The hotel was understaffed—its morning shift workers unable to commute in—and the tired graveyard shift were ordering guests not to leave the hotel. Rumors flew around that several persons had been shot on the street.

Blade went back upstairs, to the top floor pool terrace. The door was not being guarded, and he slipped out, across the terrace behind the casino, through an arcade tunnel and into Place du Casino. It looked like a ghost town. Not a soul stirred. The taxi rank across from the Hotel de Paris was deserted

Blade heard the whirring of helicopter blades, glimpsed the chopper coming his way, and he ducked beneath a Bentley, on exhibit outside the Grand Casino, until the flying machine passed. He walked around the Casino, to Avenue Ostende, and looked down into the port. The last remnants of a smoldering yacht were sinking into the sea; a speedboat whizzed outside the jetties, slowed, turned, and whizzed back the other direction.

Blade descended a set of stairs to the public *ascenceur*, and got inside the elevator, then cursed when he noticed the camera inside the moving room.

At the Sûreté Publique building in La Condamine, Furnivall's men, in the control booth monitoring the 46 cameras placed strategically around Monaco, saw Blade, and dispatched a car with two men to meet his elevator. They were waiting for him as he appeared out of the passageway connecting the *ascenseur* with Quai John F. Kennedy.

"Press!" yelled the reporter, startled by the Kalishnikov-carrying commandos. "Bill Blade—*The Miami Herald*!"

"A yank," said one of the commandos. Then to Blade, "Don't you know there's a curfew on, mate?"

"I'm a reporter. What's going on?"

"Get in!" ordered one of the Brits, gesturing to the Renault Five with his weapon.

"Am I under arrest? Where are we going?" demanded Blade. Monaco, with a crime rate comparable with Antarctica, was the last place Blade ever expected to be kidnapped. And by commandos?

"Shut up and get in—now!"

Blade climbed into the back. The car made a U-turn and drove the wrong way up the quiet quai, arriving at police headquarters in less than 90 seconds.

Blade's detention was immediately communicated to Colonel Furnivall, who consulted with Alec Perry.

"Have Blade brought here," said Alec. "We can use him to our advantage. We want the media's sympathy, not their enmity."

Blade was escorted back to the car and driven up the Rock, past the blockade and through Monaco Ville's narrow streets to the Princes' Palace, and waved through into the palace parking area.

Alec greeted Blade at the back door. "Hi, I'm Jason Meade. Sorry for the chilly reception earlier."

"Bill Blade." Blade offered his hand. "*Miami Herald.*"

"Yes, I know who you are. We are delighted to have you here," said Alec.

"You are?" Blade was puzzled. "But *who* are you?"

"I'm part of the team that has returned Monaco to the Spinola family."

"Why?"

"It's a long story Bill, but I'm going to fill you in completely," said Alec. "This is the start of an exciting new era for Monaco, and *you* are going to be first with the in-depth story."

"Uhh, why me?" asked Blade.

"Very simple," said Alec. "Because you are lucky enough to be here this morning. And between you and me"—Alec winked—"it is to our advantage that the whole truth be known about what we're doing."

Sure thing, thought Blade, who, on the surface, ate up the sugary sweet delivery.

"Why have you done this?" asked Blade.

Why? *Why* had never occurred to Alec, aside from the handsome sum he was being paid. He could not say that the Grimaldis were a bad regime that deserved to be overthrown like a tin-pot African dictator. Because, in fact, Monaco was a huge success story and its natives were well looked after. No abuse of human rights. Corruption, pay-offs, did exist—but in no greater amounts than most other places. Badness was kept at a distance; refused entry. Crime did not exist. Growth was spectacular. Infrastructure was constantly improved upon; daring new plans underway to reclaim more land from the sea. Monaco was run as efficiently as a Swiss cuckoo clock.

So it was tough for Alec to come up with a *why*. Because it's here? No. Because Barry Zubrick had been dreaming for decades about owning his own country? No again.

"For centuries," said Alec, "the Spinola family has been planning for this day. Monaco was taken from them by force. This historical struggle has been in their blood—they have strived to regain what was taken from them. Call it genetic compulsion. The Monegasques are their people. They have no plans to change the way Monaco is run. In fact, they intend to give more power to the National Assembly, make Monaco more democratic."

"Who is representing the Spinola family?" asked Blade. "Is it a direct descendant?"

"A descendant," said Alec. "He's here, in the palace. You will meet him. We're going to give you, exclusively, the first interview with Prince Spinola."

"Is he Italian?" asked Blade.

"Originally," answered Alec.

"Where has he been living till now?"

"Uhhh, New Jersey."

"New Jersey?"

"Yes," said Alec. "Many Italians emigrated to the Uni..."

"Where in New Jersey?" asked Blade. "Which town."

"Uhhh, Hoboken. As I was saying," continued Alec, "many Italian-Americans..."

"You mean he's American?"

"By birth, yes," said Alec. "But he has always considered himself *Monegasque*." Alec was starting to worry. This reporter was no fool; he was going to crucify them.

But Blade was all they had. Maybe they could offer him a job. Press spokesman. At triple his current salary. *After* his article was published.

"Is this U.S.-inspired?" asked Blade.

"Absolutely not!"

"But who is financing them?"Ever since Watergate, every investigative reporter in the United States was taught a basic principle: *follow the money.*

"The Spinola family has saved their money for centuries," said Alec. "An investment in this day."

"What is *your* background?" asked Blade.

"I am a consultant to Prince Spinola," said Alec. "I think he is ready to grant you an audience. Excuse me a minute." Alec left the room. He walked down a corridor, turned a corner and into the Prince's Bedroom, expecting to find Spinola, where he had left him catching a few zzzs. But the room was empty. He walked into the Great Salon. General Stemmer and Colonel Furnivall were standing, conducting the hustle and bustle of phone answering and manpower deployment.

"Have you seen Spinola?" asked Alec.

"No," said J.J. "We don't want him in here. We have Ducruet in the next room making up his mind."

Alec left, searched other rooms, until he came to the kitchen. Spinola was sitting on a stool at the counter, drinking from a half-filled glass tumbler, a bottle of single-malt scotch whiskey next to him.

"Hiya, Alec, wanna join me?"

"What the hell are you doing?" yelled Alec. "You can't drink now!" He picked up the bottle and emptied its contents into the sink.

Spinola drained his tumbler, taking no chances on Alec's next move.

"I'm thirsty!" yelled Spinola. "What's your problem?"

"You!" shouted Alec. "You're my goddam problem! We've got a reporter here *and* the French President, both of whom want to meet you. And you're drunk again!"

"Lithen," said Spinola, feigning a lisp. "You're addrething the Printh of Monaco. Thow thom rethpect!"

"Stand up!" ordered Alec. "I want to see you walk."

Spinola got off the stool. "Walk where?"

"Just walk a straight line. I want to see how drunk you are."

Spinola walked. It wasn't perfectly straight, but it wasn't bad.

"At least you look presentable," said Alec. "Straighten your tie."

Spinola was dressed in a three-piece pin-striped suit, black belted shoes, freshly polished, and a dark silk tie with a subdued pattern.

Alec stood back, took a critical look. "You're missing something. Let me think. A cane, that's it! It'll give you an elegant touch. Follow me."

Alec walked back to the Prince's Dressing Room, rummaged around several closets and came upon an umbrella stand with several umbrellas and canes. Alec chose an ebony cane with a simple silver knob. "Here." Alec held the cane out to Spinola. "It'll also help you walk straight."

Alec led Spinola down the corridor, back to the den where Bill Blade was waiting. "Don't talk a lot," Alec instructed. "Just answer questions—yes, no—as few words as possible. I'll fill in. Got it?"

"Yeah, yeah," said Spinola.

They entered the room. Blade, who had been sitting, scribbling into his notebook, stood up.

"May I present Mr. Bill Blade of the *Miami Herald*," said Alec.

"Good to meet ya." Spinola offered the tip of his extended cane in lieu of a handshake.

Not knowing whether to bow or laugh, Blade reached out shook the tip of Spinola's cane. After three shakes, Spinola withdrew the cane.

"I kinda like this," said Spinola. "I think I'll use it all the time." He twirled the cane in the air, got dizzy and almost tripped, then settled into an overstuffed chair. "So, Billy the Knife, what can I do you for?"

Blade looked at Alec in astonishment.

"It's the excitement," said Alec, apologetically. "And no sleep."

And a good measure of booze, thought Blade, who could smell whiskey on Spinola's breath.

"You are," said Blade, "the new Prince of Monaco?"

"In the flesh," said Spinola. "After all these years, it feels great to be home." He winked at Alec.

Alec grimaced.

"Had you ever been to Monaco before?" asked Blade.

"No, but you have to admit," Spinola laughed, "this is a helluva way to visit Monte for the first time!" Spinola slapped his knee.

Blade wished he'd brought a cassette recorder as he tried to memorize each word, his brain in a frenzy.

"Do you have other Spinola family members here with you?" asked Blade.

"Yeah, I had my cousin Vinnie here for a day, but he tried to muscle in on the action," said Spinola. "And, anyway, he don't rank—he's an Esposito, not a Spinola."

Alec, still standing, tried to cut the interview short. "The prince is tired. I suggest we do this later . . ."

"I'm not tired," said Spinola. "I just need a drink. My kingdom for a drink!"

Blade scribbled madly into his notebook. Alec moved toward Spinola, who held up his cane and held it out toward Alec like a sword.

"I want a fucking drink!" demanded Spinola. "I'm the fucking prince and I can have a fucking drink if I want one, Alec!"

"Who's Alec?" said Blade.

"Him!" said Spinola, pointing his cane. "Alec Perry."

"I thought your name was Jason Meade?" said Blade.

At that moment, Barry Zubrick walked through the door. He had been napping in another room, and now he was up, trying to find out what was going on in his new home.

Barry saw Blade first. "Oskilamala!" exclaimed Barry. "What the hell are *you* doing here?"

Blade looked at Barry in amazement, unable for a few seconds to put it together. "The real question," said Blade, "is what *you* are doing here?"

"The hell with both of you!" hollered Spinola. "I want a fucking drink!"

*****

General Stemmer thought that the French president, after 45 minutes, had had long enough to consider his proposition. He knocked, then entered the Small Salon where Ducruet and Jean-Pierre were still engaged in discussion.

"Look," said J.J. "We don't have all day. It's a mess out there. Let's add it all up, Mr. President, see what we've got if you agree.

"One, no bloodshed.

"Two, no scandal—no threat to European unity.

"Three, no resignation for you.

"Four, France makes more money out of Monaco than before.

"Five, France gets to annex Monaco in 2099.

"And six, both you and Jean-Pierre get more money than you've ever dreamed about. A half percent of Monaco's tax revenue adds up to *many millions*. What do you say, do we have a deal?"

President Ducruet spoke and Jean-Pierre translated. "Philosophically, we are opposed to your offer. It is insulting that you think you can buy a territory France has pledged to protect."

"This ain't philosophy 101," said J.J. "And we're not offering to buy shit. We have *taken* the principality. And we have taken it legitimately. And we're prepared to take our case to the UN and the International Court to have our legitimacy recognized. What we're offering here is the basis for a new treaty with France. And let me tell you, sir, if France is unwilling to deal with us, we'll sign a treaty with Italy instead. We are already in contact with the Italian government," J.J. lied.

Ducruet laughed bitterly. "I must have more time to think this through."

J.J. closed the door behind him and walked back out to the Great Salon. Colonel Furnivall was talking on his radio phones and he motioned J.J. to hold on, then spoke.

"General, we have reports that French recon planes have been flying overhead. There are rumors of mobilization in Toulon."

"Keep me informed." J.J. chomped furiously on his cigar. He marched down a corridor, heard loud voices and poked his head into the den occupied by Alec, Spinola, Blade and Barry Zubrick. Spinola was standing on a coffee table, trying to keep Alec and Barry at bay with his cane, which he swished through the air like Zorro. Bill Blade, wide-eyed and disbelieving, was taking it all in from behind a chair.

"And what the hell is going on in here?" boomed J.J.

Everyone froze. Silence. And then Spinola farted. A loud explosion that had Barry ducking for cover, believing that a gun had discharged.

J.J.'s cigar fell out of his mouth. Spinola bolted out the door. The general stooped over, picked up his cigar, then closed the door behind him. He looked at Bill Blade. "I don't believe we've met," said J.J. "I'm General Stemmer. Who are you?"

"Bill Blade, *Miami Herald.*" The reporter extended a hand.

J.J. shook Blade's hand without enthusiasm; looked first at Alec, than at Barry. "Could somebody tell me what *he* is doing here?"

"Are you the person directing this operation?" Blade interrupted.

"No comment," said J.J. "I'm not giving any interviews." J.J. turned to Alec Perry. "Would someone please tell me what is going on in here? Alec?"

"Why does everyone keep calling you Alec?" said Blade. "I thought your name was Jason Meade?"

"Arrest that man!" Barry Zubrick pointed at Blade.

Blade stood frozen, awed by the incongruity around him, and then it dawned on him.

"You're the man behind this, aren't you?" he pointed at Barry.

"Seize him!" screamed Barry.

"Ease up," said Alec. "He's not going anywhere."

"That damn reporter!" yelled Barry. "He's the man who started this whole thing!"

"What?" asked Blade, confused. "I haven't done anything . . ."

"The hell you haven't!" yelled Barry. "You wrote that damn-fool article on me and Gary Lincoln!"

"So what?" said Blade.

"So what?" said Barry. "I'll tell you so what. If it wasn't for your lying article, the police wouldn't have taken away my right to live in Monaco, and I wouldn't have even *thought* of bringing the Spinolas back. That's so *what*."

Alec sidled up to J.J. "Do me a favor," he whispered. "Get Barry out of here. I'm going to need to talk to Blade."

"C'mon, let's go," said J.J., grabbing Barry by the arm. "I've got to get back to the French president."

Blade's ear perked up. "You mean President Ducruet is *here*?"

J.J. ignored the question, put a tighter grip beneath Barry's arm, guided him toward the door.

"What about that reporter?" screamed Barry. "He knows too much!"

"Let Alec deal with it." J.J. led Barry out.

Alec and Blade studied each other.

"Well," said Alec, "I guess you know pretty much the whole story—more than you should."

"It's not my fault," said Blade, defensively. "You brought me here."

"I know, I know. We've got to work this out some-how. How would you like to become part of the team, work with us?"

Blade was silent.

"You could be press secretary to the new prince."

Blade said nothing.

"And you could earn a salary well above what you earn now."

"Is that why *you* are here?" asked Blade.

Alec didn't reply.

"I'm a reporter," said Blade. "It doesn't pay much, but that's what I am, what I always wanted to be."

"Would a hundred grand do it?" asked Alec.

Blade thought for a moment, just a moment, and nodded no. "I like my job just fine."

"You're still young, you don't understand how the world works," said Alec. "You'll work as a reporter for 20 years, be totally loyal, get paid shit, and then one day you'll make a mistake and you'll be finished, tossed out on your ass. Take the money, Bill. When this is all over you'll be able to start your *own* newspaper and report to your heart's content."

"It wouldn't be honest," said Blade.

"Christ," said Alec. "Just my luck to come across the *one* honest reporter in the world. All right, forget the job, be a reporter. Let me pay you to walk away from this story, to pretend you were never up here."

"I can't do that either," said Blade. "I came here to do a piece on Barry Zubrick. This is the biggest story of my life."

"But we can't let you just walk out of here, report that Prince Spinola is a drunk, a puppet for Barry Schwartz."

"So what are you going to do," said Blade. "Kill me?"

10

Gerry Spinola found a stock of liquor inside an antique china chest and marveled at the top shelf names: Macallan, Laphroaig, vintage Armagnac, Chivas Regal—his favorite. He uncapped a bottle of Chivas, took a long swig. What he needed was a quiet room where he could sit and contemplate his new home over half a bottle of liquid gold. At the end of the corridor, a door was slightly ajar; he peeked in, it looked cozy, a quiet niche where he could lose the others, and himself, for an hour or more. Spinola swung the door open wide—and came face to face with President Ducruet and Jean-Pierre Grazin, the minister of state, who had been sitting, whispering, and who now both gaped at Spinola, carrying a cane in one hand, a bottle of chivas in the other, and his fly undone.

"Who the hell are you?" demanded Spinola of the two startled, distinguished-looking men.

Jean-Pierre spoke. "This is the President of France, Jacques Ducruet. And I am the minister of state. Remember?"

"Well, howdy-doody, guys. Good to meet ya. I'm Prince Spinola. Welcome to my palace."

Jean-Pierre translated. Ducruet gasped.

"Care to join me for a shot of whiskey?" asked Spinola. He put down his cane, uncapped the bottle and took another long swig. "Ahhhh, that's very excellent. With booze like this around, I think I'm gonna like this place. Whattaya say, youz guys wanna moisten your gobs?" Spinola thrust the bottle. Ducruet recoiled in horror.

Ducruet spoke rapidly and Jean-Pierre translated. "This is no way to conduct yourself in front of the President of France."

"Hey, if you don't like it," said Spinola, "you can suck my dick!"

Jean-Pierre didn't translate, but glared at Spinola as he took another swig.

"If you will please excuse us, we are having an important discussion," said Jean-Pierre.

"This is *my* fucking palace," said Spinola. "*You* find another room."

There was a knock on the door, then General Stemmer entered. Spinola clumsily capped the bottle and shoved it down the front of his trousers.

"What are *you* doing here?" boomed J.J.

"I'm trying to get these frogs to lighten up," said Spinola.

J.J. strode to Spinola, grabbed him by the arm, and walked him toward the door. As he did this, the bottle of Chivas slipped down Spinola's trousers and out a leg, shattering on the marble floor, forming a puddle.

"Shit!" yelled Spinola. "Look what you've done!"

J.J. squeezed Spinola's arm tighter and dragged him from the room. "What the hell do you think you're doing?"

"All I wanted was a quiet drink!" yelled Spinola. "I'm the fucking Prince of Monaco and I can't even have a drink in my own goddam palace!"

Barry Zubrick, at the other end of the corridor, ran up to them.

"What's going on here?" snapped Barry.

"Your `prince' just disgraced himself in front of the French president," said J.J.

"I can do what I want," yelled Spinola. "This is *my* fucking palace."

"This isn't your palace, you, you statzi-moo!" yelled Barry. "This is *my* palace."

"Whattaya mean, your palace?"

"You're just a figurehead," said Barry. "A puppet, remember? I pull the strings around here. The palace is *mine*, not yours. I'll rent you an *apartment* to live in."

"Fuck you!" yelled Spinola. "I'm outta here!"

Jean-Pierre stood only yards away, listening through the door, cracked open an inch.

"Shhhhh!" J.J. scolded. "Keep it down." He pointed at the door. "The French president is in there."

"Get this moo-brain out of here," ordered Barry.

"Who are you callin' a moo-brain?" yelled Spinola.

"You, you moo-brained stalimatzi!"

Spinola lunged out at Barry with a right to the jaw, merely grazing him, but Barry, a frail man, reeled back onto the floor, holding his chin.

J.J. loosened his grip on Spinola and ran to help Barry get up; Spinola ran down the corridor, in search of the china chest and another bottle.

J.J. led Barry to the Great Salon, the operation command center, where Colonel Furnivall was still presiding over a battery of telephones, static and radio. J.J. set Barry down in a chair.

Colonel Furnivall looked up. "The old Prince of Monaco is on the phone again—he's holding for the president."

"Okay," said J.J. "Wait five minutes then channel the call to the den."

J.J. returned to Ducruet and Jean-Pierre, who were now sitting back in their chairs, agitated, impatient.

Ducruet spoke rapidly, loudly, in a confrontational tone, and Jean-Pierre translated.

"So, this is your prince, your figurehead? You wish to make me the laughingstock of France, of the world?"

J.J. considered the question, remained calm, spoke slowly. "If you see it that way, then you must choose. Laughingstock or disgrace."

"But this is a farce," Ducruet protested. "We cannot give the principality to those fools."

"I'll say it one more time," said J.J. "We're not asking you to 'give' anything. We have already retrieved what rightfully belongs to us. We are asking for a treaty. You have our terms. If you don't wish to begin a negotiation, we will negotiate elsewhere, starting with Italy."

"And follow through with your threats, your black-mail?"

"You bet," said J.J. "We'll need *something* to take the media spotlight off us, and that'll work swell."

Ducruet grunted, collected his thoughts. "Let us be hypothetical for a moment. Suppose we were to agree to this change in power—make a 'treaty,' as you say. And let us suppose we do so in the historical context you suggest. The ancestor of your Spinola owned only the Rock, Monaco Ville—that's all there *was* back then—so we are *only* talking about the Rock, not Monte Carlo, not the port, not Fontvieille. Right?"

J.J. considered this for a moment. It wasn't much, but they were getting *somewhere*—a step in the right direction. "Go on, hypothetically," said J.J.

"Monte Carlo was not created, not built until the 1850s, almost 600 hundred years after the Grimaldis took power. Fontvieille, on land reclaimed from the sea, is practically brand new. And even La Condamine was nothing but wild land, bushes and trees for centuries. For the Spinolas to claim *anything* beyond the Rock would be preposterous, pure piracy."

"Hold on a minute," said J.J. "If the Spinola's had the opportunity to determine their own destiny in Monaco, who's to say they wouldn't have developed the principality the same way, or even better? And then—hypothetically, of course—there's a case for charging the Grimaldis 700 years rent for use of the Rock."

"It would be for a court to decide," said Ducruet. "Are you prepared to abide by the ruling of a court on this matter—on the whole matter of your coup d'état?"

"I would have to discuss this with Prince Spinola," said J.J.

Ducruet laughed contemptuously. "And something else," he said. "Again, hypothetically, if you were given territorial rights to the Rock, it would be imperative that you return to the Grimaldis all their personal possessions: the precious family heirlooms, paintings, antiques, jewelry, furniture—everything."

"The Grimaldis," said J.J. "were able to assemble their collection only because of their stronghold on the principality. Many of their personal possessions, I'd venture to guess, were *gifts* to the principality. Had the Spinolas not been uprooted, *they* would own this collection today, and the Grimaldis would be scattered around."

As Ducruet began to speak, the telephone rang, answered by the minister of state. "Prince de Monaco," he said to Ducruet and passed the phone to the president.

Ducruet listened, said a few words, listened, grew agitated, uttered a few heated words, and the call ended.

Jean-Pierre said something; Ducruet held up his hand to fend off questions, put his hand over his eyes, rubbed them, and collected his thoughts.

"The Prince of Monaco is angry," said Ducruet, translated by Jean-Pierre. "He is threatening to mobilize his own men and attack if France does not act by noon. And he says he will sue France for all costs, all losses."

Ducruet addressed Jean-Pierre, asked him not to translate: "Maybe that's the answer. France can settle with the Grimaldis, pay them off." He turned back to J.J. and Jean-Pierre resumed a translation. "We are, hypothetically, talking about real estate only: the Rock. And the natives of Monaco Ville must be given a choice, to remain or to move. If they choose to move, they must be paid a fair market value for their property."

J.J. jotted everything down on a yellow legal pad. "And what about Monte Carlo and the rest of Monaco?"

"France would take control of everything except the Rock which, as you stated, would become the property of France in the year 2099. As for personal property of the Grimaldis: an independent assessment would be made and the possessions would be divided equally.

"It is still hypothetical," continued Ducruet. "But it is the best I can do."

"I need to meet with my associates," said J.J., not wishing to provoke Ducruet's contempt by mentioning Spinola by name.

J.J. went to find Barry Zubrick in the Great Salon.

"Barry, I think we're on the verge of something," said J.J. He outlined the proposal, reading from his legal pad.

"That's no good," snapped Barry. "Monte Carlo is where all the money is made. Those thieving frogs—they're trying to use us to take Monaco for themselves!"

"Look at it this way," said J.J. "The Rock gives you the territorial independence you want. You get your own country, guaranteed till 2099, like you wanted."

"Without the revenues of Monte Carlo, the Rock means diddly-squat," barked Barry. "Admission fees to the hokey wax museum and the Oceanographic Museum add up to noodles. And if we don't have access to the port—if it's owned by the French—they'll be able to strangle us with God knows what kind of taxes and conditions. And then there's SBM. I want control of SBM. And I'm sure, by their calculations, SBM goes hand in hand with Monte Carlo."

"Well, they're ready to deal," said J.J. "Let's give them *something*."

"Tell 'em they can have Fontvieille," snapped Barry. "That place is nothing but a mosquito-infested sewer."

J.J. wrote down Fontvieille. "Half ownership of SBM."

"No way!" snapped Barry. "Sixty-forty, my favor."

Alec Perry appeared at the door. He was pale, perspiring, a cold sweat.

"Alec, you look like you've just seen a ghost," said J.J.

"Spinola's dead," whispered Alec.

"What?" said Barry.

"Spinola, the dentist. He's dead," said Alec, louder.

"What are you talking about, dead?"

"Dead. Dead," said Alec. "How many times do you want me to say it?"

Barry froze. "You mean *dead*, really dead?" His voice grew meek. "Did you kill him?"

"Follow me," said Alec.

Barry and J.J. followed Alec out into the corridor, around a corner, out of the private apartments and into a more formal section of the Princes' Palace. Alec led them into the Throne Room, an ornate, arched room, richly decorated with frescoed ceilings. On one side, opposite an extravagant marble fireplace, sat the throne, framed by burgundy velvet curtains and gold tassels. And upon the throne sat Gerry Spinola, tilted to one side, his mouth agape, his eyes wide open, his hand reaching down to the floor toward a bottle of Chivas Regal, fallen from his grip. The liquid gold was forming a large dark stain on the red velvet carpet beneath the throne. Behind Spinola was the Grimaldi coat of arms and the motto *"Deo Jevanti"*—Latin for God Willing.

"Is he dead?" barked Barry.

J.J. took Spinola's pulse. "Yeah, he's gone."

"How?" asked Barry.

"Probably a cerebral hemorrhage or a stroke from the look of him," said J.J.

The full impact of a dead Spinola was only beginning to dawn on Barry.

"Holy Malola! What are we going to do now. Alec?"

"We need a descendant, a relative. He has a couple of ex-wives. I can't remember, did he ever say if he had any children?"

"No," said Barry. "But he mentioned a nephew, a stockbroker, the one who gave him our ad in the *Journal*."

"Was his last name Spinola?" asked Alec

"I don't know, he didn't say. What about Vinnie, his cousin?"

Alec rolled his eyes. "Not a chance." He thought a

moment. "There's only one thing we can do: pretend Spinola is still alive, at least until we have a signed treaty with France. *Then* we'll worry about a successor. C'mon, let's get that mess cleaned up."

Alec walked close to Spinola, closed his eyelids over his eyes. He tried to pop his mouth closed, but the jaw wouldn't budge.

"Let's set him up straight," said Alec. "We're going to have to present Spinola to the minister of state. The minister has to swear his allegiance to Prince Spinola to make it official."

Spinola's face was already white and clammy.

"We're going to need some make-up," said Alec. "J.J., get one of your men to rummage through the bathrooms—there must be pancake or rouge somewhere. Then get back to the president. Make the best deal you can. We need to act fast."

"Wait a minute, wait a minute," said Barry. "I don't want a lousy deal out of this."

"We don't have any choice," said Alec. "We need any deal we can get. J.J., do it!"

Alec looked at his watch; it was just before 11 a.m. "At noon precisely, we swear our allegiance to Prince Spinola. Now let's get him ready."

*****

J.J. walked back to the private apartments, to the Small Salon where Prime Minister Ducruet and Jean-Pierre were waiting.

"Gentlemen," said J.J. "We are willing to make some concessions based upon your proposal..."

"Hypothetical proposal," corrected Jean-Pierre.

"Yes, *hypothetical*," said J.J. "We are prepared to return half of the Grimaldi treasures to the Grimaldis. On the issue of territories outside of the Rock, we are prepared to concede Fontvieille, and to give France a forty percent share of SBM holdings."

"You mean two-thirds of the sixty percent of SBM controlled by the prince?"

J.J. was confused, not familiar with SBM shareholdings, and he didn't want to get into details now. "Yes, that's right," he said.

Jean-Pierre translated.

President Ducruet folded his arms and shook his head defiantly as he listened. Then he spoke and Jean-Pierre translated.

"On the subject of the territories, the Rock is all we can allow. It satisfies the historical claim you make and it should be enough."

"But there are no revenues on the Rock," protested J.J.

Ducruet considered the point. "We could, hypothetically, come to an arrangement on SBM so that *some* hotel and casino revenue would go toward the upkeep of the Rock. But your so-called prince should be responsible for developing his *own* enterprises."

"Access to the port is another concern to us," said J.J. "700 years ago the Spinolas had complete access. If France takes possession of La Condamine, we will be subject to its whims."

Ducruet pondered the problem. "France could make a special allowance for access to the port." Ducruet paused. "My personal considerations aside, I think we are being generous. If these conditions are unacceptable to you, I have no choice but to accept the fate your blackmail may bring."

"How about shared control of Monte Carlo and La Condamine?" asked J.J.

"The Rock only," said Ducruet.

"I'll consult with the Prince," said J.J. "If he is agreeable, can we be more than hypothetical and draft an agreement?"

"If we must," said Ducruet.

J.J. walked back to the Great Salon. Barry wasn't there, and Colonel Furnivall appeared alarmed.

"We have reports," said Furnivall, "that a force of men led by the old prince is preparing an assault from the mountain."

"Where?" asked J.J.

The two men huddled over a large map of Monaco and neighboring territories, the Alps Maritimes, that was spread over a dining table.

"Here and here," said Furnivall, pointing to two mountain approaches from Beausolei into Monaco on side streets.

"Where are the soldiers from?" asked J.J.

"Off-duty constables and carabiniers who live outside of the principality."

"How many?"

"Between two hundred and two hundred fifty."

"Arms?"

"Whatever they've been able to muster. Rifles, pistols, shotguns."

"We're on the edge of an agreement with France," said J.J. "We have to stall them. Bloodshed will spoil everything." J.J. paused. "And that's what they want: martyrs, for the media to focus on."

"Keep them at bay and hold fire," J.J. called, as he walked out the room. Down the corridor, around a cor-

ner, back to the Throne Room, where he found Alec and
Barry fussing over Spinola's corpse, trimming his hair,
applying pancake to his face, painting his blue lips with
a thin layer of lipstick.

Barry turned and faced J.J. "Well?" he snapped.

"On the question of territory they won't budge,"
said J.J. "It's the Rock and only the Rock."

"Masalabahd!!" yelled Barry. "The frogs are so damn
stubborn. The hell with 'em!"

"No," said J.J. "Let's not bite our nose to spite our
face. We've got this far. You've got a country, even if it's
only the Rock. I'd say that's quite an accomplishment.
Now, we've got to get this thing ironed out quick because
the old prince has put together a small army and he's
planning an attack. If there's fighting, casualties, dead
people, this whole thing's going to come crashing down
on us. The old prince knows this. His strategy will be to
get a few dead Monegasques on camera, evoke the world's
sympathy and get us compared to Saddam Hussein. We've
got to make this agreement with France and let *them*
handle the old prince.

"Here's what Ducruet is willing to do," continued
J.J. "Share SBM-Monte Carlo revenues . . ."

"How much?" asked Barry.

"Enough for the upkeep of the Rock while you de-
velop your own enterprises."

"They'd have to define an amount in writing," said
Barry.

"Okay," said J.J. "Next, they're willing to offer
unconditional access to the port, tariff free."

"How about shared control?" asked Barry.

"I suggested that. No way."

Barry considered the offer. "Can't we counter again?"

"We don't have time," said J.J. "We could lose it all. Go for it. Take the Rock. We can quickly sign a letter of intent with Ducruet and negotiate the small print later. Then we can call our troops to the Rock, a natural fortress, and avoid armed confrontation with the old prince."

"Okay," said Barry. "Do it."

*****

Across town, Bill Blade was filing a world exclusive to his newspaper in Miami. Forty-five minutes earlier, Alec Perry had written Blade a note extending the reporter free passage through Colonel Furnivall's roadblocks, and Blade had made his way back to Loews and telephoned the *Miami Herald*, telling incredulous editors that the supposed new "Prince Spinola" was an American, a drunkard from New Jersey, and that the money, the brains behind the coup came from Barry Zubrick, another American, an expatriate millionaire whom the paper had tied to con-man Gary Lincoln one month before, the very man Blade had traveled to Monaco to speak with.

And then Blade composed his inside story of a coup d'état in the Mediterranean paradise of Monaco, and he read it over the phone to a copy-taker:

> Dateline Monaco.
>
> This fairy-tale principality on the French Riviera was this morning rocked by a coup d'état. English mercenaries working for Barry Zubrick, an American multimillionaire resident in Monaco, seized the tiny principality in the middle of the night and sealed off its borders.
>
> Zubrick was exposed by this newspaper one month ago for conspiring with Melbourne-based

con-man Gary Lincoln to defraud investors in a
scheme called 'Liberty is Us.'

Zubrick's plan is to install a puppet prince
named Spinola, a native of New Jersey who bears
the same last name of a man who ruled Monaco
over 700 hundred years ago.

Zubrick and his men have occupied the Princes'
Palace on the Rock and are negotiating with French
President Jacques Ducruet, who flew in hours after
the coup to meet secretly with the coup plotters.

The precision, military strike, which took place
at 1 a.m. local time, was engineered by retired
American four-star General John. J. Stemmer.

The principality is calm, quiet—a curfew is
being strictly enforced. But there is chaos outside
Monaco's borders, where traffic has been building
for several hours. The roads for miles around are
completely blocked.

There are no reports of casualties. A pleasure
yacht hit a mine, one of many that have been
planted around Monaco's two ports. It has sunk.
It is unknown how many persons were on board
or if they escaped the blast.

This reporter was this morning escorted to the
Princes' Palace and witnessed firsthand the dis-
array and confusion of the conspirators. The so-
called 'Prince' Spinola appeared to be drunk and
incoherent.

The Royal Family was at Roc Agel, their country home in the mountains near Monaco, during
the siege of the palace. They are said to be safe,
and there are rumors that the prince will attempt
to regain the principality by force.

Guests at the four-star deluxe Loews Hotel are shocked and amazed by this military action in a principality thought, until this morning, to be one of the world's safest havens.

Blade made good on his promise to omit Alec's name from all reportage on the coup.

Knowing that his story was en route, the *Miami Herald* held its presses and Blade's scoop appeared in the later editions as a front page headline: "Coup in Monaco— The Inside Story."

*****

Sitting with President Ducruet and Jean-Pierre, J.J. drafted a letter of intent which, in simple English, stated the basic tenets on which both parties agreed:

1. France will recognize the territorial integrity of Prince Spinola, contingent upon a decision in Prince Spinola's favor at the International Court at The Hague.

2. Prince Spinola's territorial claim will be limited to the Rock, Monaco Ville.

3. Prince Spinola will be permitted a percentage of the shares of SBM, thus providing him with a revenue from Monte Carlo's hotels and casinos. It would only apply to those shares controlled by the government of Monaco. The percentage should be no more than 45 percent and no less than 25 percent; the exact figure to be determined by the International Court.

4. Prince Spinola will be permitted unconditional access to the port.

5. The value of all Grimaldi personal possessions will be independently valued and shared equally between Spinola and the Grimaldis.

6. Any natives of Monaco Ville who wish to leave will be allowed to do so; they will be paid a fair market value for property.

7. Monaco Ville will revert to French rule in the year 2099.

8. In all other ways, the 1962 French treaty with the Grimaldis of Monaco will transfer to Prince Spinola.

Jean-Pierre re-wrote the draft in French, which Ducruet read slowly. Then the President drew an S.J. Dupont lacquered ball-pen from his inside coat pocket and, with a flourish, signed the French document, then the English version. He passed his pen to Jean-Pierre, who witnessed the agreement with his own signature.

J.J. stood up. "I will get Prince Spinola's signature and then you will meet him."

"We'll come with you," said Jean-Pierre. "Let's finish this business."

"Be patient for just another few minutes," said J.J. "The prince is resting."

J.J. closed the door behind him, walked quickly to the command center in the Great Salon. He took the fat, unlit cigar out of his mouth and threw it across the room. "It's done!" he boomed.

Colonel Furnivall looked up, still talking into a phone. "We're about to be engaged by the enemy—what do we do?"

"Pull back, pull back!" yelled J.J. "Bring everyone home—to the Rock, Barry Zubrick's Rock!"

Furnivall spoke quickly into the telephone, put it down, picked up a radio-phone, issued more commands. CNN cable news was blaring in the background on a large-screen TV set.

J.J. left Furnivall to coordinate the retreat to victory. He walked out, down a corridor and around to the Throne Room. Alec and Barry were still posing Spinola's corpse.

"We've got a signed agreement!" hollered J.J. "All we need is Spinola's signature."

Barry grabbed the papers, English and French, put on his glasses and read the English. Then he pulled a Bic pen from deep within a trouser pocket and signed "Prince Spinola I." J.J. counter-signed as witness.

"Let's wrap this up," said J.J. "I'll get Ducruet and Jean Pierre—meet you in the command center in five minutes."

*****

Alec and Barry stood formally in the command center, Furnivall still barking commands, as J.J. led President Ducruet and Jean-Pierre Grazin into the large, high-ceilinged room. Introductions were made by J.J. without explanation, and during a pause that followed, their attention was diverted to the TV set and CNN's announcement that "We are cutting live to Bill Blade in Monte Carlo. Bill is a reporter for the *Miami Herald* and he is on the phone with us. Bill, what exactly is happening in Monaco?"

Barry was in shock, couldn't contain himself. "Skamalibard! What the hell is *he* doing on TV?"

Alec looked sheepish. Jean-Pierre held up his hand to stop the talking, he wanted to listen, and, as he did, he translated for President Ducruet.

"As I exclusively reported in the *Miami Herald* this morning," said Blade. "The man behind the coup is an American named Barry Zubrick."

"Holy Malola!" shouted Barry.

"Who is Barry Zubrick?" asked Jim Mooney at the CNN anchor desk.

"He is a reclusive multi-millionaire and so-called 'freedom-fighter.' Last month my newspaper implicated him in an international fraud called 'Liberty-is-Us'."

"I'm going to sue!" yelled Barry. "This is slander!"

"Shhhh!" admonished Jean-Pierre. "We can't hear."

"Barry Zubrick has a history of wanting to create his own country," Blade continued. "He tried to do this about ten years ago in Australia. It appears he is using some kind of historical justification for taking over Monaco, using a man named Spinola, who is from New Jersey."

"Don't go away, Bill," said the anchor. "We need to go live to Hoboken, New Jersey, to our correspondent Frank Martin. Frank, what have you got?"

"Jim, I'm here with Vinnie Esposito, who is Gerry Spinola's cousin. He tells me that Spinola is a practicing dentist in Hoboken, that when he works it is mostly on welfare patients. Vinnie, what more can you tell us about your cousin?"

"Yeah, yeah, my cousin Spinny ain't a bad guy—he just mixes with the wrong people," said Vinnie. "And anyway, his name ain't really Spinola. Our grandpop's name was Spinolini."

Barry Zubrick saw it coming. He charged the TV. "Oskilamola!" he yelled. Barry pushed the Grundig TV off its stand and it crashed to the floor, blowing the picture tube and shattering the screen. It was unnecessary. Jean-Pierre could barely understand Vinnie's thick New Jersey accent.

"C'mon, let's go see the Prince," huffed Barry; Ducruet and Jean-Pierre stood frozen in astonishment. It took them a few seconds to regain their composure, then they followed Barry, Alec and J.J. down the long corridor and into the Throne Room. Prince Spinola was primped upon the gilt throne, upright, majestic, eyes closed.

The men lined up before Prince Spinola; Ducruet and Jean-Pierre stood uncomfortably.

J.J. pulled the draft agreements from inside his jacket and presented them to the French president. "Prince Spinola has signed the agreement," said J.J. "We ask that the minister of state swear his allegiance, as is customary, to the new prince."

"Is he asleep?" asked Ducruet; Jean-Pierre translated.

"No!" snapped Barry. "The prince is meditating. It has taken centuries for him to arrive at his proper royal status. He is finally home."

At that moment, Spinola's nose began to bleed. It dripped slowly at first, then gushed over his lips, onto his suit.

Alec nudged J.J. in the ribs, whispered, "Even dead, this guy's a jerk."

President Ducruet stamped his foot. "This man looks like he is dead." As Jean-Pierre translated Ducruet's words, the president abruptly marched to Spinola and put his open palm before Spinola's nose and mouth. "*Morte!*" Ducruet announced.

Ducruet turned to face the group, crumpled up the agreement and threw it to the floor.

"I've had enough of this nonsense!" yelled Ducruet. "I will allow you to leave with your freedom—that is all!"

"But we have a written agreement!" yelled Barry. "You can't reneg!"

"At best," said Ducruet, "you have a dead prince. May I ask, does he have any children?"

Barry, Alec and J.J. looked at each other, shrugged. Barry spoke. "What does that have to do with anything?"

Ducruet bent down and retrieved the crumpled document. "May I refer you to point eight of our agreement: `In all other ways, the 1962 French treaty with the Grimaldis of Monaco will transfer to the Spinolas.'

"That treaty states," continued Ducruet, translated by Jean-Pierre, "that when the royal family fails to provide an heir by direct promigenture, Monaco reverts to France. And so I'm sorry, gentlemen, any way you look at it, you have no further claim to the Principality of Monaco."

"What the hell are you talking about?" yelled Barry. "We're here. We have an army. We're in control, and we'll fight to keep it!"

"On what grounds?" asked Ducruet.

"I have an agreement with Spinola!" barked Barry. He pulled from his back pocket his one-pager, signed by Spinola, conferring rulership of Monaco to Barry Zubrick.

Jean-Pierre translated the document to Ducruet.

Ducruet laughed. "This is meaningless without an heir."

"Now, wait a second," J.J. spoke up. "We are in command of the Rock and we haven't come this far to simply walk away. And, remember, there is also the Hades Covenant to consider."

"Before, you were pirates with a rationale—an interesting historical question," said Ducruet. "Now you are just pirates. Terrorists. Blackmailers!"

"Call us any names you want," said J.J. "But you're going to need a better solution than just offering us freedom. Otherwise, we'll stay and fight. You will put people at risk—everyone on the Rock—and risk destroying the palace's priceless collections."

"You believe you can take on the French army, navy and air force?"

"And do you believe," said J.J., "you can survive the Hades Covenant? If you push us into a corner, that will be our first line of defense—direct to CNN."

The room turned quiet while President Ducruet considered his dilemma.

"This is all about Monsieur Zubrick's desire to rule his own country," said Ducruet. "Am I correct?"

J.J. nodded.

"I think," said Ducruet, "I have a solution."

One Month Later

It was business as usual inside the Principality of Monaco. Engineers and laborers hammered grandstands and bleachers into place for the annual Grand Prix. The Grimaldi flag fluttered high over the Princes' Palace.

Meanwhile, twenty-five miles west, on a small island within sight of Cannes, French President Jacques Ducruet presided over a ceremony that would transfer Ile Saint Marguerite from French rule to the newly-named Zubrick's Island, a quasi-independent state protected by France.

Eight of Colonel Furnivall's men, standing ankle deep in bird droppings, formed a short gauntlet as Prince Barry of Zubrick's Island sloshed through the mire onto a make-shift platform.

Nearby, General J.J. Stemmer chomped on an unlit cigar, trying to ignore the stench of fresh guano. Alec Perry and his new bride, Isabelle, held their noses and applauded in quick rotation as President Ducruet hung a large medallion around Barry's neck, all the while trying to suppress a cunning grin.

For the French president had neglected to mention why the Ile Saint Marguerite was not already inhabited: Years earlier, with French permission, the UN had declared the tiny island an international bird sanctuary, protecting the annual migration of African birds to and from the European mainland.

The digestive processes of these feathered tribes assured that Ile Saint Marguerite was liberally coated with bird dukey year-round.

The *Miami Herald* received a Pulitzer Prize for Bill Blade's investigative reporting. Gary Lincoln was indicted for fraud. Alec Perry and General Stemmer collected their success fees and were appointed Honorary Consuls-At-Large for Zubrick's Island.

And last seen, Barry Zubrick was busy questioning fertilizer executives on the feasibility of removing knee-deep deposits of guano without disturbing the nesting grounds of his loyal and protected subjects.